Treasure Maid

Kendra Dartez

ISBN-13:
978-1502768704

ISBN-10:
1502768704

DEDICATION

For Ruth Worley, my beloved grandmother and my biggest fan. Thank you for reading my first draft when I was a young girl and telling everyone I would be published one day!

CONTENTS

ACKNOWLEDGMENTS

I am so grateful to my mother Linda Fulks and to my sister Sara for reading and helping edit my book. Your attention to detail and support helped turn my childhood dream into a reality. Thank you to my husband Josh for always encouraging me to write, even when I had writer's block and lack of sleep from staying up with our young children. And of course, I would love to acknowledge my sweet children for reminding me of the joy that comes with imagination and storytelling.

CHAPTER ONE

The dark night seemed to swallow Becky Blake as she stared out at the winding, moonlit road. Her world had changed in just a few months. At thirteen, she suddenly found herself alone. She couldn't believe that both of her parents were gone. Her father, a fisherman, had been lost at sea, and her mother had died shortly after giving birth to her baby sister. Becky burst into tears thinking of her poor mum who was now in heaven. And then her grief turned to anger at her Aunt Matilda. Aunt Matilda had split her family and scattered them about England. The older ones were sent to work and the younger ones were sent to live with Aunt Matilda at her Cornish home and tavern in Mevagissey. Her twin older brothers Richard and George, age 17, were sent to sea, her sister Susannah, age 16, was sent to a textile factory in London, and she was to work as a maid at an estate in Derbyshire called Kendree Hill. Aunt Matilda had told her that the older siblings' wages would help pay for her younger siblings: nine year old brother Jack, seven year old Katie and Baby Lisbeth, but she knew better. The wages would go straight into Aunt Matilda's pockets.

The driver interrupted her thoughts, "We're here, miss!" he called from outside. Becky Blake wiped her gray eyes with her sleeve and grabbed her trunk. Her mother had always told her to be proud of her family- proud of her Scottish name. She smoothed down her jet black hair, stuck out her chin, and opened the carriage door.

She glanced out at the massive castle like building. Even in the dark, the mysterious and enormous house scared her. She had never seen such a sinister place. She shuddered, but again, did not want the driver to see her. The driver, a young man who also worked at Kendree Hill, grabbed her trunk. "You'll be wanting to see Mrs. Jordan, the head housekeeper. But since it is so late, Miss Effie, the cook, can show you to your rooms," he said in a gruff voice.

Becky jumped as a shadow tapped her shoulder. She turned to see a plump young woman, "I'm Effie! Follow me!" She followed her into a dark kitchen- she couldn't see much because it was so dimly lit and also because Effie whisked her up a side set of servant stairs. She counted- they climbed up three stories to a cramped attic room with three cots. "Here's yours. Pleasant sleep…we'll be getting you up before sunrise, so get some sleep then," Effie said cheerily.

It was too dark for Becky to even see who else shared the room with her and Effie, so she just collapsed onto the cot with her clothes still on. When she dreamed that night, she dreamed of her mother kissing her on the cheek. "Goodnight, dearie," whispered her mother's ghost.

CHAPTER TWO

Becky sighed as she gazed at the packed shelves in the Kendree's pantry the next day. She envied her employers for everything from their rich clothes to their huge mansion. She learned from Effie that the Kendrees had lived in Derbyshire as one of the most wealthy and prominent families for generations. The castle like house stood overlooking the countryside from its far away hill. Even though she came from a working class family, Becky knew she would have trouble being a prim and proper little maid. At the age of thirteen, she had been called spirited. Her wide set gray eyes constantly shifted around the kitchen. One of her faults was being clumsy which always seemed to get her into trouble. In fact, she already had fallen down the stairs in the morning and managed to break a piece of china at high tea. Becky Blake, in short, was all thumbs. Her older brothers had always laughed and her mother and father thought it was cute, but somehow she thought it would get her canned, especially here. She had always longed for adventure, but suddenly being on her own in the new place made her even clumsier. She hated and feared and yet was intrigued of this new life all at once.

Most of all, she really missed her family. She wondered what her sister Susannah was doing in the textile factory. Did she feel the same? Was she lonely and scared? As she stood in the pantry, she again envied the Kendrees for their wealth- "just look at all of the food," she thought. She also thought that if she had just a fraction of their wealth, she could be with her brothers and sisters.

She resented the job, but there was some pleasure in that she did not have to endure Aunt Matilda's snide comments. "Look at you!" she had sneered as she had seen her off, "You are just like your father- always putting on airs and yet look where that got him- at the bottom of the sea!" Becky was not sure why she said she had been putting on airs- perhaps, it was the fact that she had stuck her chin out in defiance when her aunt told her she was not to wear the broach her mummy had given her. "Where you are going, you might get that stolen…best kept with me," her aunt had said.

Becky's thoughts came back to the present as she heard Effie call to her. She placed a jar of pickles she had just canned on the shelf. "Coming, mum," she answered and walked quickly out of the pantry.

"I need help with these afternoon tea dishes," Effie said.

"Yes, mum," Becky said and walked towards her. Just as she stepped onto the cold tile floor, a giant honey colored mastiff came barreling into the kitchen, knocking Becky down. The dog did not bark or bite, but a very large bit of drool slobbered down on Becky's cheek. She yelled at it in a rage," Back dog!" she shouted.

She heard a boy call distantly, "Boris! Boris!"

Effie laughed and reached out a hand to help her to her feet, "I see you met the beast Boris! He loves to eat some of the scraps…and between you and me," at this point she winked, "I think he prefers us to his master…the young Master Edwin." She pointed toward the kitchen door leading to the dining room. "Best you take the beast back to him…I already have been told to stop overfeeding him."

"Yes, mum!" Becky actually loved the big dog- it had just caught her off guard. She pulled at the big dog's collar, "Come now, Boris, let us find your master." She and the dog walked through the kitchen and up the stairs, following a rather annoyingly high pitched boy's voice. She gawked at the large oak dining table and pale blue wallpaper as they walked through the dining room and into the grand foyer. The foyer was green and gold and had a wide staircase that twisted around and around. She had to practically push the mastiff up the stairs, which took quite a long time. She finally reached the top and hurried down the hall to her left. The boy's voice was closer now. She followed the shrieks until she stopped in front of a room. She knocked quietly. She did not want to be called out for knocking too loudly or for entering without permission. She straightened her new maid uniform as best she could and tried to wipe off the dog drool too.

"Come in!" shrieked the boy. She entered the boy's room. And as she did, she saw the young boy who was to be her master. A boy of about twelve or thirteen with dirty blond hair and rosy cheeks sat at a desk playing with toy soldiers and yelling "Boris! Boris!" over and over again.

She had to clear her throat. He looked up and laughed, "There he is! I wondered how long it would take someone to bring him!" Becky had to suppress her thoughts of his idleness. She bit her lip. Her mummy had always told her to watch her temper.

"Who are you anyways? I've never seen you before!" he said and squinted at her as he spoke.

"My name is Rebecca Blake. Becky that is. I just started today and had the great honor of meeting your fine dog. The beast knocked me down and slobbered me." He raised an eyebrow as she spoke, "Oh no!" she thought, "What did I do wrong now?"

"Are you making fun of my dog?" he questioned. "Come, Boris!" he suddenly tried to speak in a commanding voice. He scratched his dirty blond hair in frustration when the dog remained standing next to her.

"No, sir," Becky said and her eyes flared up.

"Well, get out! Go clean up the stairs or something! I suppose he drooled all over them!"

"No, he did not."

"How dare you contradict me. I bet you don't even know how to read and write, and yet you dare to talk back to me!"

His words stung Becky's heart. She did know how to read and write, but it wasn't her fault she did not know more. She had been forced to stop her education when she was of age to work. She remained in the room and said very calmly and bravely, "I do know how to read and write. My parents are dead, and I must now work to support my family."

The young master Edwin stared at her a long while, shocked that she had not left and even more shocked that she had spoken back to him. He finally spoke, "Well, no more schooling sounds like a treat...I will overlook your disobedience since you are clearly addled in the head. Also, you did bring me my dog when the others wouldn't....how did they die?"

This was her turn to be shocked, Becky bit her lip to stop the quivering, "My father was a fisherman...his boat was lost at sea. My mother died when my baby sister was born."

"Lost at sea! Do you know anything about sailing? I am quite fascinated with it," Master Edwin went back to thinking of himself; his momentary interest in her parents' death had passed. Becky could not believe how quickly the topic changed, but was grateful because she did not want to cry in front of him.

"Well, I know a thing or two," she said, "My brothers are sailors now. They are both working on a ship in Her Royal Majesty's Navy."

"Fascinating!" the boy tossed his soldiers. "I would love to take a ship. I only rode on a small one to cross the channel to go to Paris."

"Well, sir, I better be going before the cook misses me," Becky said. She patted Boris on his head and walked toward the door but turned, "If I am excused?"

"Yes, maid, you are excused," he said pompously and then added, "but I do hope to speak to you more about seafaring."

Becky thought she would be glad to leave his room, but as she exited, she realized it was good to speak of her parents. She had not told anyone else- not Effie the cook or Mrs. Jordan the housekeeper. As she went down the staircase, she realized that the foyer had gotten darker as the evening approached. Soon someone would light candles, but not yet. She shuddered as she walked down the stairs this time and yet did not know why. Her father always had told her that she was like him- odd that when Aunt Matilda said that she meant it as a complaint but when her father had said it, he had meant it as a proud compliment. He used to say that she had his premonitions and to always trust them. Well, as she walked down the winding staircase, she felt a spark of fear mingled with adventure. Why, she was not sure. But at least it was a different feeling than grief.

CHAPTER THREE

Besides walking to Master Edwin's room, Becky had stayed in the kitchen and helped Effie for most of her duties. She was glad that Effie seemed to be in charge of her that day, for Mrs. Jordan looked gloomy as well as the other three maids she had encountered. Later that evening, while carrying dishes up to one of the footmen, she peeked through the kitchen door and into the dining room and saw a young woman who appeared to be Mrs. Kendree talking with an older, cross looking woman. A distinguished looking man and Edwin also sat around the table waiting on their dessert course. She closed the door and walked back down to where Effie was finishing her éclairs. "Who are the two women in the dining room?" she asked.

"Shouldn't be espying, Becky, but….that would be the young Mrs. Kendree, and the old Mistress Kendree."

"The young one is lovely! Is that Edwin's mother then?"

"Yes, it is. It seems Young Master Edwin has left an impression on you?" Effie smiled mischievously.

Becky did not like the way she was looking at her, so changed the subject, "I loved your éclairs you made tonight!" she said.

"Why thank you, Becky! Next time just say so, and I'll make some extra for you!"

"You can…I mean the Kendrees will allow it?" Becky was trying not to get into any more trouble.

"Of course! How do you think I got so fat?" Effie bellowed. Becky and Effie both giggled. It was the first time Becky had since her mummy's death.

One of the footmen, Andrew, came into the kitchen, "Master Edwin asked for a Becky Blake?"

Effie laughed, "Best be going, miss!"

"Edwin Kendree- he's one spoiled little boy," Becky whispered. Effie gave her a worried look and shook her head at her as a warning.

"Don't let anyone in there hear you say that," she said.

Becky picked up her skirts and ran. She opened the door

and quietly stepped into the room.

"Yes sir?" she said and remembered to lower her eyes and curtsy as Mrs. Jordan had told her to do that morning.

"Fetch my coat and dog and have him ready to go in a few minutes. I wish to go for a walk instead of dessert," he ordered.

"I'll get your coat sir, but the dog? Again?" she asked and had to bite back her sarcasm.

"You speak to my son like that? My word, what a feisty little maid we found," Master Kendree questioned, yet followed the question with a robust chuckle.

"I am sorry, sir," Becky said and knew she should have stopped but got up the courage to say, "But I have already gotten Boris for him once today and was scolded for messing up my uniform. I apologize, sir."

"Do not apologize, child. Edwin should not be using you as his valet. But you do have a lot of spunk…just like your mother," Master Kendree said, and as he said it Becky looked up sharply.

"You knew my mother, sir?"

"Why didn't you know? That is how you got the job. Your mother and your Aunt Matilda used to work at our northern estate."

"No sir, I did not know," she muttered and could not believe her ears. Suddenly, she looked around and felt closer to her mother somehow.

"Why yes. And as for Mrs. Jordan, do not worry about what she says of your uniform. I am, after all, the head of this manor." Master Kendree went on, "And the dog is quite gentle. But still, do not worry about fetching him. Boris is Edwin's dog. And besides, Edwin did not ask permission to skip the dessert course."

"Thank you, sir," she said and almost turned to leave.

"You may leave, Miss Blake," Master Kendree said and chuckled again. Becky turned and nearly bounded back into the kitchen.

"What happened to make you in a hurry?" Effie asked.

"I almost got myself into a lashing, so I thought anyways,"

Becky replied.

"Is that so!" Effie laughed. "I suppose there is a lot more we need to teach you." Becky smiled at Effie.

Afterwards, Becky and the three other maids got ready for the dessert. Julie, who was nineteen and the one closest in age to Becky, brought up the éclairs. Miss Cackle, an old snippy looking woman, brought up two pies, and Mrs. Bob helped Effie clear the dirty dishes from the last course.

"Becky, carry up the custard, please!" Effie called to her.

Becky picked up the custard. The other two maids had already stepped out of the way and were letting Becky through to deliver the custard to Andrew to serve to the Kendrees. All of a sudden, Becky slipped and fell on the floor with the bowl of custard covering all of her hair and face.

There was a sudden snide laugh coming from Edwin and a large commotion of laughter. Effie and Mrs. Bob even ran to the door to peak through to see what the fuss was about.

Then a shrill voice stopped the laughter, "Get up! You are

such a clumsy disgrace!" the young Mrs. Kendree yelled.

"Now, Alice," Mr. Kendree interrupted. "It is her first day. Why I almost slipped on that very same rug the other day…"

"James, leave this to me! You, Rebecca, have destroyed more things on your first day than any other maid has ever done in their entire stay! You are dismissed!" she huffed.

"Yes, mum. I am truly sorry. It…it won't happen again," Becky faltered.

"You do not understand me. There will not be a next time. I am dismissing you from this house forever!" Mrs. Kendree hollered.

Becky's eyes started to water. "Oh, mum, I'll do anything. Please…please don't dismiss me. I need to work for my family…"

"My decision is final! I will not allow such rude, clumsy…"

"Please! I promised my mother to help take care of them…especially baby Lisbeth! I'll do anything…scrub the floors, work the gardens…" Becky cried.

"Now…let's not be rash!" the old Mistress Kendree spoke

for the first time, "I will not allow such a hasty dismissal of one of our maids!" she boomed. The two Kendree ladies glared at each other, but the young one lowered her eyes in defeat.

"Very well…I will see to it that Mrs. Jordan keeps you out of sight of me and of my guests and away from expenses. Why, you are not supposed to even be in this dining room…only the footmen! Now leave! Andrew, clean up this mess!" the young Mrs. Kendree stammered.

"Oh, thank you!" Becky said with relief. Becky ran back to the kitchen where Mrs. Bob was finishing up the dishes.

"Close one, eh? Not as lovely as she looks is she," Mrs. Bob laughed in a whisper, "never seen such a *lady* in a fit" she whispered into Becky's ear.

Mrs. Bob had beady eyes and close tiny eyebrows. She was a petite woman and Becky already at thirteen towered over her. Her thick, dull brown hair had wisps of gray hanging from a loose bun. "I remember," she was saying, "when I was young and slipped and tumbled. Oh, my mistress was furious. Ah, but I learned after that.

And so will you. So will you."

"Yes, I think I probably have learned my lesson," Becky replied while wiping custard from her face. She had learned to steer clear of the young Mrs. Kendree.

CHAPTER FOUR

A couple weeks passed rather uneventfully for Becky, but one day she was so delighted to receive a letter from her sister Susannah. The old butler Mr. Roberts brought it in to her, and she tore it open in the kitchen right in front of Effie.

Dearest Sister,

Times are very hard here at the factory. I work all day and have very cramped rooms at night. The mistress in charge said she thought I would only last a week, but so far I have proven her wrong. My fingers are small and fast, so I get more done than most of the other girls. I do so miss you, but I do not know how or when we will see each other next. Everything I make is sent to Aunt Matilda. She says she may find something for me closer to her home, so I can help with her tavern too, and I do hope so. I am very tired. All my prayers are with you.

Your loving sister,

Susannah

Becky wiped her eyes from the tears. Effie stopped what she was doing and walked over to Becky. "From your family?" she asked.

Becky nodded. Just then the sour faced Julie showed up, but she barely noticed Becky had been crying. In fact, she barely seemed to notice anyone. "Miss Effie, mum, the elder Mistress Kendree would like to see Becky. Why, I would never know. She's in the library." Julie said.

"Me? But why?" Becky questioned. She had tried to avoid the Kendrees as much as possible since the incident with the custard.

"Well, you better be off then," Effie said. Becky tucked her letter in her apron pocket and walked out of the kitchen and up toward the east wing where the library was located. Becky knocked on the door to the green library and walked in. Every time she entered the room, she was taken aback by the menacing family portrait starting at her from over the fireplace. The man in the painting had mocking big, dark eyes and a harsh line of mouth. Something about him made her cringe. She forced herself to look away from it and turned her eyes toward Mistress Kendree instead.

"Becky Blake!" Mistress Kendree exclaimed. "I have wanted

to talk with you."

"Yes," Becky curtsied and put her head down.

"You probably are wondering why? Well....I have important news. It has come to my attention that my deceased daughter's children have become orphans. Their father was killed in the American war between the states."

Becky looked up, "I am sorry, mam," she managed to say.

"I thank you...it seems that there is nothing to do but to bring them here. That is where I want you to come in. I want you to be my granddaughter's personal maid. She is twelve. It will be more responsibility, but I am sure you will do fine. Your mother was one of the very best we ever had, so I have high hopes for you," the old Mistress Kendree said.

Becky just gaped at her. She had given her mother a compliment, but she was worried about being a personal maid. She was not trained for that sort of thing. "Yes, mam. Is that all?"

"Is that all," Mistress Kendree smiled a slow smile, "I am sure that Mrs. Jordan will update you on everything. And Becky...never you mind what the other Mrs. Kendree said to you a fortnight ago. Remember, I am the original lady of this house."

"Yes, mam. Thank you," Becky said. Becky had to fight back a smile too. She was beginning to like the old lady of the house. Just then Zachery Perkins, Mr. Kendree's valet, came into the library. He was a lanky young man with dark wavy hair and blue eyes. Becky secretly thought he was extremely good looking.

"Mistress Kendree, Mr. Kendree would like to see you," he said dutifully without even looking Becky's way.

Mistress Kendree simply nodded regally and dismissed him with a wave of her gloved hand. She looked back at Becky and winked, "My dear, run along and find Mrs. Jordan. You will have a lot to learn before my granddaughter arrives."

As Becky turned to leave, she tripped over a stack of books on the floor. She heard Mrs. Kendree laugh and thought she caught a smile from Zackery. Mortified, she stooped over to pick up the knocked over books. On top, there was a book entitled *Pirates of England*. Now who would be reading that? Probably Edwin. He had said he liked the sea, she thought. Becky fixed the stack as she had found it and quickly left the room. As she hastily walked away, she wondered about the book. It was a subject that always intrigued her as well. Her father had told her several stories. The next time she saw Master Edwin she would have to ask him if she might be able to borrow it.

That night, Becky had another vivid dream. This time she was on a ship with her father. Oddly, it was not a fishing boat but a Ship of the Line. Her father was at the mast yelling out orders. Suddenly, a huge, dark wave of water swept up on the deck and washed her over. She woke up with a start gagging. Effie was shaking her gently.

"Can't we get any sleep around here?" she heard Julie sigh from the bed in the corner.

"Leave her be," Effie said.

"Sorry," Becky put her face down in her pillow and tried to get back to sleep.

The next several days, Mrs. Jordan trained Becky on the etiquette of being a personal maid when she was not busy with her many other duties. It was now the beginning of summertime, so Becky hated working inside all day. She missed the outdoors terribly, but she simply had no time to explore. Sometimes, when she was washing some of the windows, she would get a peep at the beautiful rolling hills and sometimes catch a bird in mid song. But those days were rare, for she mostly had to finish scrubbing the floors downstairs, and she also had to work on the upstairs bedrooms getting them ready for Mistress Kendrees' grandchildren. She really disliked working with Miss Cackle. Miss Cackle, despite her name, had no sense of humor and really seemed to go out of her way to chastise Becky. Becky just had to bite her lip and bear it. And Julie, who always seemed downcast, seemed even more so after hearing of Becky's swift elevation to lady's maid.

Today, Becky had just finished mopping the kitchen floor, "Effie," she said leaning on the mop, "Why are you cooking such a huge meal today?"

"Well, I thought you would have heard! The Kendrees relatives are coming today!" Effie shrugged as she labored over some dough.

"Oh…" Becky said.

"Didn't Mrs. Jordan tell you?" Effie asked.

"Yes, but I had lost track of the dates," Becky said. It was true; she had thought they were not supposed to come until the following week. Becky was nervous; however, a part of her was excited to meet the girl she would be spending so much time with. Henrietta, was it? And her older brother would be coming too. She hoped he was not as annoying as Edwin.

Just then, Julie came into the kitchen, "Becky! What are you doing here? Mrs. Jordan wants us both upstairs prepping the rooms for the new master and mistress!" Julie said.

"I see. Do you know how long it will take them?" Becky asked.

"Well, they should be arriving sometime this evening," Julie answered.

"But what time?" Becky asked again.

"Look, I don't have time for questions. We have work to do," Julie said briskly and walked to the laundry.

"In a bad mood, that one," Effie said.

"Do you know what they are like? The girl and the boy?" Becky asked.

"No. I don't believe they have ever been here. Of course, I have not been here for very long. Just a couple of years. But their arrival means extra mouths for me to feed, so I need to hurry too." She busily went about the kitchen.

"Where did you come from before working here?" Becky asked.

Effie looked up, "Well, when I was fifteen, I got a job at an estate helping the main cook in the kitchen. My papa insisted that I go and work for this rich family. I worked there about seven years but they got rid of me..."

"Why would anyone ever get rid of you?" Beck couldn't believe it.

"Who knows with employers? They must have had financial woes, but they did write me a lovely recommendation which sent me here," Effie said.

"I see," Becky replied.

"Well, enough questions. Aren't you supposed to be helping Julie?" Effie said, "Run along. Best to make a good impression this evening."

"Yes," Becky smiled and left the kitchen in a hurry. She was just finishing up her chores for the day, when she heard the foyer's doorbell ring. Mrs. Jordan had told all of them to meet her at the bottom of the stairs to greet the new arrivals. She quickly dashed down the front foyer, forgetting she was not supposed to use it. Thankfully, she did not fall and actually got there before Mr. Roberts, the butler, opened the door. She slid into place beside Effie and Julie. All of the servants lined up to greet them. Mrs. Jordan was first in line, followed by Miss Cackle, Effie, Julie, Zackery, Andrew and Basil, the footmen, and the gardener Mr. Parish.

The Kendrees all arrived from the east wing as well. Old Mistress Kendree wore a fine golden taffeta gown. The young Mrs. Kendree looked absolutely beautiful in a dark blue gown, and Mr. Kendree wore a fine suit. Edwin stood sulking behind them, probably mad that they had made him wear his Sunday clothes, Becky thought. They all really did look splendid.

The door opened. "Mr. Timothy Hargrove and Miss Henrietta Hargrove," Mr. Roberts, the butler, announced.

Becky followed suit as everyone on the staff curtsied or bowed. Becky caught a glimpse of the girl she was to work for personally. Henrietta was simply beautiful. She had thick, golden hair with blue, delightful eyes. Her brother was quite handsome. He had wavy dirty blond hair and teasing blue eyes as well. He looked to Becky to be about her twin brothers' age or maybe even older.

Mrs. Kendree pulled Edwin out to greet them formally. And Becky noticed that Master Kendree greeted the boy with a strong handshake and the girl with a nod. Old Mistress Kendree broke the etiquette by hugging the girl to her with tears in her eyes. Becky thought that was quite touching and felt that they really should have been left alone. She stared at the two children and could only imagine how they were like her in that their parents were also now gone. How different their worlds were though- these children could live comfortably with their grandmother, aunt, uncle, and cousin, yet her brothers and sisters and herself had been split up and sent to live in differing directions. She was deep in thought when Mrs. Jordan broke her out of her trance, "Becky, show these two to their rooms. Timothy's is right next to Edwin's room and Henrietta's is as you know, in the blue room."

Becky nodded and picked up her skirts.

"Follow me," she said. They were halfway up the stairs when Timothy broke the silence.

"Aren't you a bit young for a maid?" he asked, "I was hoping for someone older and prettier," he said.

Becky was shocked. "Ah, no sir, I mean…I am old enough to work."

He just snickered at her. They walked down the hall and stopped in front of Timothy's room. "Here it is," she said and waved him into the room. He opened the door and stepped inside without another word.

Becky breathed a sigh of relief and walked Henrietta to her bedroom. "Here's your room, Miss Henrietta."

"You can call me Pearl. It's my middle name," Henrietta said as she stepped into the blue room.

"Yes, miss. Do you need anything before I go?"

"No, not yet, I mean...I want you to keep me company," Pearl quickly said.

"Yes mam," Becky said as she watched Pearl make herself comfortable in a rocking chair.

"I can't believe I'm here," Pearl said.

"You lived in America?" Becky questioned; she felt comfortable with this girl.

"Savannah! My daddy died last month. Oh, I hate those wretched Yankees!" Pearl said.

"My father died too. So did my mum," Becky said quietly.

Pearl glanced up at her, "When?" she asked.

"A few weeks ago," Becky said. "Are you alright, miss? Do you need a handkerchief or something?"

"Well...well...I don't need your pity! Get out!" Pearl suddenly screamed.

"Yes, miss," Becky said. As she closed the door she could hear the girl sobbing.

CHAPTER FIVE

Becky's duties doubled as she now had to attend to Pearl. Pearl would be nice to Becky, but sometimes she would suddenly snap that she was doing something wrong. Still, for some reason, Becky seemed to understand that Pearl was not angry at her in particular. Becky knew she was angry for the same reason as she was. They both missed their parents terribly. One such outburst of Pearl occurred several weeks later. Becky had brought up Pearl's breakfast from the kitchen when she had rudely shouted, "No! I wanted two lumps of sugar in my tea! Why can't you get it right?" Pearl said and shook her head in agitation. Just then the door opened, "Aunt Alice!" Pearl said with a sudden smile.

"Now what is all of this fuss about? Is the girl doing something she should be punished for?" The Young Mrs. Kendree asked and looked sternly in Becky's direction. But much to Becky's surprise, Pearl had said no.

"You may leave us, Becky," Mistress Alice said. Becky had started to call her Mistress Alice (or Mistress Malice) in her head, depending on her mood.

She nodded and left the room; however, out of curiosity, she did not leave the hall right away.

"Well, my dear niece, I have decided that you are entirely too lonely out here. It is about time you meet some of your other relatives from England. Who would you like to meet first? I shall write to them immediately," Mistress Alice said.

"No one, Aunt Alice! And I am not lonely. You must not worry," Pearl said quickly.

Becky left the conversation since it was not about her as she had thought it might have been, and because she remembered how her mother had said it was not polite to eavesdrop. She wondered why Pearl would not like to meet her relations? She pondered this as she walked down the hall and toward the servants' stairway.

When Becky returned to the kitchen, she found Effie wide eyed. "What is it, Effie?" she asked.

"My cinnamon bread is half eaten. Who do you think did it, Becky?" Effie asked.

"I don't know…" Becky said, looking at what was left of the loaf of bread.

"At first I thought it could be a rat, but the piece missing is too clean cut," Effie shrugged her shoulders, "Then I thought that Edwin might have come down here for a midnight snack last night."

"Probably, I've seen Edwin eat twice as much before," Becky said.

"I hope so…" Effie said. She turned back to her morning pastries. Becky wondered why Effie sounded scared when she said it.

"Who do you think did it?" she dared to ask.

Effie turned quickly and raised an eyebrow, "I just have been hearing things the last few nights…footsteps…that sort of thing. I know it is probably just that Edwin or Timothy, but still it is scary to hear footsteps in the middle of the night. I never heard them before in the years here."

Becky had never seen Effie scared before, and for the first time she realized that she was not the only one in their little servant room that had trouble falling asleep.

"Now don't you worry," Effie said and laughed it off. "Look at me upsetting you for no good reason. Off you go! Take these pastries and get ready for the morning tea." Becky nodded and soon forgot all about the missing bread as she was soon consumed yet again with work.

Later in the week, however, she remembered the missing bread as soon as she saw Effie's disturbed face. Becky immediately asked, "What's the matter?"

"Some of my blueberry muffins went missing. I just don't understand it," Effie frowned but seemed to shake it off. She shrugged, "Don't worry. I will have to discuss it with Mrs. Kendree is all. I was hoping not to. Can you be a dearie and fetch me some more flour from the pantry? I suppose I should make some more instead of crying about it."

"Of course, Effie!" Becky said exuberantly for she wanted to help Effie with her problem. Becky opened the pantry door and stepped into the wide room. Jars of honey, sugar, flours, canned jams, and lots more filled up the white shelves. It was a very long pantry. Becky scooped some flour out of the barrel and was about to leave when something moved in the left corner. Becky started backing up, thinking it was a mouse when to her utter surprise a girl popped out of the dark corner.

"Ah!" Becky exclaimed and brought a hand to her mouth in fear. But as the figure turned to her, she realized it was Pearl. "What are you doing here?" Becky gasped.

"Shhh!...Be quiet...I've found a secret passage," Pearl whispered excitedly in her funny accent.

"A what?" Becky asked and then quickly added, "Are you sure?"

"Yes, I mean, that is how I got here. I went through it already. Here, I'll show you," Pearl said as she tugged on Becky's sleeve.

"Wait! Effie's in the kitchen. Let me tell her where I'm going," Becky explained.

"No! Don't tell anyone! Just meet me in my room upstairs in a few minutes, but hurry, all right?" Pearl demanded.

"I'll try to hurry, but I do have some more chores to do if you don't want me to let on that something odd is going on," Becky said firmly.

"Yes…yes…just hurry!" Pearl said and disappeared under the back corner of the shelves.

Becky's hands shook with excitement as she scooped up the flour for Effie and went out of the pantry.

She went about helping set up for the morning tea for the two Mrs. Kendrees and Mr. Kendree. As soon as she was finished, she slipped away. Once she was on the stairs, she broke into a half jog. She might be clumsy, but she was very fast. She could beat some of the boys in her fishing village in a foot race- skirts flying. She ran up the stairs and flew open the door to Pearl's blue room and was utterly surprised to find Edwin sitting on Pearl's bed.

"Why are you here?" Becky asked, out of breath.

"Me? The real question is why are *you* here?" Edwin asked haughtily.

"She told me to come here," Becky spoke back. She did not

know why, but holding her tongue was hardest with the bratty Master Edwin than with the others.

"Well, I suppose you know that we found a …" he stopped and lowered his voice, "a secret passageway?"

"You know too?" Becky asked. She was both surprised and disappointed. She had hoped that Pearl had only wanted to keep it a secret with her.

"Of course I know! We both found it!" Edwin snipped.

"Well, I didn't know that," Becky muttered. Then she added, "Well, where is it?"

"Just close the door, and I'll show you," Edwin ordered.

Becky closed the door and turned around, "Well? Where is it?" she demanded.

Edwin walked over and lifted an old blue rug up. Beneath it was just the plain oak floor, or that's what Becky thought at first glance. Edwin removed a loose plank of wood, then reached his hand through and pulled on a handle that was attached to a nearby wall beneath the floor. He pulled again, "It must be jammed," he said in an irritated voice.

Becky stood back up, "What is the handle for anyway?" Becky questioned but almost as soon as she asked, the floor started to shake, "What? OHHH!" Becky screamed as she fell through the trap door and onto a wooden stairs just a few feet below. They both rolled a second or two down the old stairs. When they finally stopped, Edwin answered Becky's question.

"That…is what the handle is for."

Becky stood up and balanced herself against a dirty stone wall. Her skirt was ripped at the bottom of it. She glanced around. It was extremely dark. Her eyes followed the swerving staircase made of rickety wood. Becky bent over to get a better look at her skirt when suddenly Edwin yanked her hand, "Ouch! Oh…don't you know that hurts! I have bruises all over me!" she snapped.

"No, I didn't! Hurry up!" he said looking over his own bruises and scrapes.

"Well, yes, I am coming," Becky moaned. They continued

down the twists and turns of the staircase. Along the way, Becky saw a woman's shadow ascending higher and higher. Becky froze. "Is it a …..a ghost?" she dared to breathe.

Edwin began to laugh, "No, you strange, stupid girl! It's only Pearl," He let out one last chuckle as Becky watched Pearl step out of the shadows and reach them on the stairs. She had a lantern in her hand, so Becky could now see what a large rip she had really gotten on the skirt of her uniform. Mrs. Jordan, the housekeeper, will be so angry with me, she thought.

"What happened to y'all? Why, you're absolutely filthy!" Pearl exclaimed.

"The trap door delayed again," Edwin explained.

"Again!" Pearl said.

"Yes, and please, let's get out of this dirty passageway!" Becky half demanded. She picked up her ragged skirt and turned around to go back the way they had come.

"No! Not yet" Pearl said excitedly, "I've found some peeping holes! Follow me!" she turned around and went back down the old stairs.

"Peeping holes!" Edwin said. He looked at Becky, and they both shrugged and followed Pearl. When they reached the bottom of the stairs, they walked down a very long, narrow hallway. When they caught up with Pearl, she was sticking her face up against the dirty old wall.

"What are you doing?" Becky exclaimed.

"Come closer...it's the library...and there are people in it...three...maybe four...I've never seen before," she whispered.

"Let me have a look!" Edwin said rather loudly.

"Shh! Fine...just be quiet," Pearl said as she lifted her face away from the two holes just big enough for a person's eyes. Edwin then stuck his face to the wall. Becky watched with her mouth open in shock.

"But...can they see him from the library?" Becky asked. She was suddenly afraid of why there were peeping holes and more importantly, why there were strange people in the house.

"Simple," Edwin answered, "The holes are in the painting of my great, great grandfather Sir Frankford Kendree. When you are not using the holes, you slide this piece of wood and move it over the holes," He picked up the piece of wood and showed it to Becky. Painted perfectly there were the pair of chilling dark eyes. She knew which painting they belonged to- the only one in the house that had scared Becky.

"Oh, I know what painting this is!" Becky suddenly gasped. She felt the hairs on her arm rising in alarm.

"Yes, the painting is dated back to 1704…around the year this portion of the house was added on…" Edwin explained.

"How do you know all of this?" Becky asked.

"I'll tell you later…I promise…but first why don't you have a look?" Edwin suggested.

"Wait…I think I lost my head cap to my uniform…"Becky suddenly realized. "Let me go back for it. I am already going to be in so much trouble." Becky rushed back along the passage. "I'll come back to your room later…" she added over her shoulder as she ran. She did not want to look. She was too frightened. Suddenly, she heard a footstep behind her. Becky jumped in fright...When she turned around, there was a shuffling noise. Becky stopped in her tracks. The noise stopped too. Becky stood frozen in her fear. It was dark, extremely dark. Becky looked about herself. Cobwebs were everywhere, hanging thickly like heavy, dusty curtains in an abandoned house. Becky's hands started to shake. Her mouth quivered and her throat went dry. Then something moved right next to her. "Help me!" Becky screamed. When she turned, all she saw was a dark shadow disappearing ominously from the passage.

CHAPTER SIX

Becky quickly got hold of her senses and turned around to make her way back to Pearl and Edwin. When she reached them, everything seemed normal; Becky was ever so glad to see them. Pearl ran to meet her, "Oh, Becky, was that you who screamed? I'm terribly frightened too. I…I just don't know what we are going to do!" she hysterically whined.

"What happened?" Becky asked. She glanced back down the dark hallway. Edwin was still peering through the holes. "Edwin, what happened…Edwin!" Becky whispered rather loudly.

"Be quiet!" he said and then turned back to the holes again.

Becky sat down on the filthy floor, "Pearl," she said calmly, "Pearl, will you stop crying and just tell me what happened? Please?" She put her arm around her to comfort her the way her mother used to do.

"I wasn't crying…I am just in shock. You see…we just discovered another secret…somewhere there is hidden treasure!" Pearl said nervously but there was a streak of determination in her eyes.

"Treasure? Wait…first there is a secret passageway and then there is a peeping hole…and now there is treasure? This is a crazy game you are playing…" Becky said and as she said it her hairs on her arms stood on edge. "And if it is real then…it can only lead to trouble!"

"Oh, what a lily liver you are! I was not finished. This is no game. Now shush and listen," Pearl flopped her golden curls away from her face. "In the library Edwin saw three men huddled around an old man. Edwin told me to take a look, so I looked through one of the holes and Edwin looked through the other. I saw the oldest, ugliest man I've ever seen. He was wrinkled and so skinny…almost like a skeleton. He was the only one we could really see because the others were facing him and not the portrait. Anyway, the old man was saying that his great grandfather had been Sir Frankford Kendree's right hand man. And then he whispered something that Edwin and I couldn't quite make out, but then one of the men said loudly, 'Well, where is the treasure?' Oh, and Becky, he sounded so cruel when he spoke. Then the old man started talking about Sir

Frankford Kendree again…and he said that he was known to fund ships to act as pirates to acquire all sorts of booty….I can't believe that could be true…After all, he is one of my ancestors…" Pearl paused as if she just had thought of that, "But he said that supposedly Sir Frankford Kendree hid some of the treasure because he did not trust his men…and there was also some suspicion of his involvement in piracy. For whatever reason, he hid the treasure temporarily but was murdered before anyone could ever discover the location of his treasure. The only reason the man is here now is because he came across his great grandfather's journal that led him here…Can you imagine? We have to find the treasure before they do!" Pearl was out of breath after relaying everything they had heard.

"We have to tell your aunt and uncle at once! They need to be warned that these men are in their house!" Becky said fearfully. She had never been comfortable in the grand house and felt a sudden need to get out of the passageway. She wondered what her father would have done…but only temporarily because of what happened next.

Edwin suddenly turned around, "The men are gone and by

what they said they are coming in here. This must be where they are going to hide- surely they won't steal anything during the daylight," he said. He looked worried…"and I think I know what they are looking for! We have to get back. I'll explain later." Both girls looked at him, puzzled by what he had said. "Come on!" he said rather harshly and pushed through them and marched back the way they came. Becky looked at Pearl only for a moment and ran after Edwin, easily catching him. She heard Pearl following them at a distance, for she was not as fast.

"We need to tell an adult," Becky panted.

"No! I don't want to show anyone this yet! And…I don't think those men can find the treasure. For to find the treasure they need some kind of a map. I don't know why I am wasting my time explaining this to you now," Edwin retorted.

"And why not tell an adult that you trust! If you don't, I will tell your father," Becky said.

Edwin grabbed Becky's arm fiercely and just glared at her. Becky did not quite understand the boy, but she did think deep down that the boy might want to give his father a reason to be proud. In some odd way, he wanted to solve this before the other men. Becky did not want to play along with his dangerous game. She struggled to break free of his grip, but he held her tightly.

"Don't you forget that you are just a maid. If you tell, no one will believe you," Edwin said, "You are so stupid and ignorant…"

"Let go of her arm, Edwin," Pearl spoke from behind them. She had finally caught up with them.

"Just do not tell anyone, understand?" Edwin said and let go of her arm. Becky was absolutely disgusted with him.

"Let's get back to my bedroom. Oh, I hope you didn't lock the latch back! We might have to go back to the kitchen and who knows where the other passage those men might have found…" Pearl said and looked around nervously.

"Of course we didn't," Edwin said. Suddenly, they heard footsteps from down the passageway.

"Quickly!" Pearl whispered. "And Edwin, we need to tell your father when we return."

Edwin nodded. The three followed Pearl back to the trap door. Edwin put his hands out to help Pearl jump up back into her bedroom. She struggled up and finally swung her legs up and over. "You're next, hurry," Edwin said.

Becky flushed and stepped into his hands to get the boost. She was stronger than Pearl and easily swung up into the bedroom. She was used to swimming and climbing about her father's fishing boat. She quickly turned around and saw Edwin's panicked expression.

"Hurry, I hear them," he whispered. Becky lay down and put out her strong right arm. He grabbed it with momentum and kicked against the wall beneath and grabbed onto the side of the opening with his other arm. Becky helped him up and rolled him over. Pearl quickly closed the plank of wood and pressed a lever to close it. She then placed the rug over the secret trap door.

"How about putting something heavier over it?" Becky asked. The other two nodded.

"My hope chest...it is still full," Pearl said quickly. They pushed it over the trap door.

Becky stood up after that was done. "Do you think they heard us?" she asked.

"No," Edwin said, "I think their footsteps would have quickened...they did not seem to be in a hurry. I bet they have been hiding there and then sneaking out through the kitchen when everyone is asleep."

Suddenly a dog barked and everyone jumped. Becky saw Boris the mastiff come in the room and felt the dog's huge slobber on her face. She swiftly wiped it off as best she could.

"Well, let's go tell your father," Pearl said. "Perhaps, he will know what to do."

"Yes, I suppose you are right," Edwin said. "But I need to get something from my room first," he dashed away before either girl could say anything.

"Well, where is he going? We need to tell Master Kendree, so he can block off the other passage entrance!" Becky said as she jumped up. How could he just run off like it was a game? She was highly irritated with him. Pearl just shrugged and got up too.

As the two girls were just leaving Pearl's room, followed by Boris, they almost ran right into Edwin who had a stack of books in his hands.

"Reading?" Pearl asked.

"Yes, what are you doing playing with books at a time like this?" Becky asked. She was so furious and had clearly forgotten her station yet again, but what did that matter, she thought, if they were all in danger?

"This is what they are looking for!" he said smugly. "I was interested in sailing, and so I got these from the library the other day. I also came across this…"

He showed them an old leather journal which inside said the name *Sir Frankford Kendree*.

"Well, put the other books away! This is all we need!" Pearl exclaimed. "He must say something about where the treasure is!" Becky was not listening to the two of them at this point. Her fear and her intuition told her something bad was going to happen if they didn't tell someone quickly. She continued on down the stairs without them. But she heard Edwin saying, "Yes, I think I'll put this in my pocket for safekeeping until we see father. The servants must not be trusted. In fact, I don't know why you told her anything."

"I had to," said Pearl, "she saw me in the pantry…"

"You didn't have to tell her why," Edwin said. Becky continued on, but she felt terrible to have them discussing her. Of course, no one really knew her here anyway, but it still angered her to be thought of as a low life who could not be trusted.

They walked into the foyer and saw Julie. "There you are!" she said irritably. She glanced shrewdly at the three of them. "Master Kendree wishes to speak to all of you…in the library," she said with a humph. "He also said that I need to take Boris for a walk!" she grabbed the dog's collar and pulled on him. Boris barked as Julie pulled him along as she walked the other way.

"Good!" Edwin said but then glanced at Pearl. "What do we say?" he asked.

Pearl said, "We tell him of course. So what if they find out

55

we've been taking pastries. Those men seem dangerous."

Becky suddenly figured out why Edwin had not wanted to tell his father. He and Pearl had been the ones sneaking into the kitchen at night and swiping some food. Of course, it made sense. Becky followed the two of them to the east wing. The library door was closed. She hesitated and stopped while the other two walked through the doorway.

To her horror as the door opened, two men grabbed at Edwin and Pearl. Becky backed up and turned to run, but then someone's hand grabbed her shoulder and another hand went to her mouth. She was trapped and kicking as the captor pushed her into the library and closed the massive door.

"Don't say a word, lad," a rough voice came from the man that held Edwin.

Becky looked down at the hands that were holding her arms. They were youthful looking hands. Becky squinted at the men who were holding Edwin and Pearl, but they wore their caps low and had their head down, preventing their identities.

Just then the one holding Edwin was talking to the other one in a low tone. "Yes, yes," he yelled and then laughed and threw off his cap. Becky gasped as she looked at the man. He had no hair and an earring in his ear. The nose on his face was long and pointed. His eyes were a grotesque, pale blue color. The man holding Pearl was enormous and had dark red hair. Suddenly, a familiar voice spoke out. The voice belonged to the man holding Becky.

"They are all just children. No need to hurt them!" the voice said, "They won't say a word if we scare them enough."

Becky didn't like the conversation. The three men were plotting out what was to become of them! She looked over at Pearl who was beginning to cry and then over to Edwin who looked helpless.

The man took his hand off her mouth for a second. She saw her opportunity, "Help!" she screamed but the hand went quickly back to her mouth. It might not be heard by anyone as not many people were likely to be on this end of the house at this time of day.

The man holding her whispered, "Becky, it's not going to help. Just stay quiet and do as you are told."

"How," Becky tried to say but couldn't since the hand was still over her mouth. How did he know her name? And yet the voice was very familiar. As she was thinking, suddenly she saw Pearl kick at a large lampshade. The big redheaded man slapped her in the face with his backhand, and she started to cry again.

Edwin wiggled free for a second but only for long enough to shout, "Leave her alone!"

Becky too, wiggled, but to no avail. She was trapped. And then she heard her kidnapper say, "Well, well, Hinistrosa! What should we do with these three children?"

CHAPTER SEVEN

Becky looked away in fear, for she was suddenly facing the ugliest, old man she had ever seen. He had bushy eyebrows, leathery wrinkled skin and pale brown eyes. Despite his age, he had thick, curly hair underneath a bowler hat. The old man sat in one of the large chairs. He waved his hand at them.

"You…ha….you think," the old man started in a thick Spanish accent but then let out a series of raucous coughs before going on, "you think…I'm weak. Don't you!" he gasped for breath as he spoke and then laughed and coughed at the same time. No one answered him. Becky could see that Edwin was glancing at the easiest way out- there was a door to an outside courtyard from the library. Pearl was just crying the whole time. Becky tried to think as she stared at the portrait of Sir Frankford Kendree.

"Well, now…I can assure you that I am not weak…I hope you do not doubt me…it would be a terrible mistake to not fear the name Eduardo Hinistrosa!" he wheezed. With that he waved to his men, "Release them…they will not dare run!"

The man holding Becky released her and the others did the same. Becky took a step toward the outside door. Suddenly, the old man turned violently toward her. "Get back!" he bellowed in his raspy voice. Becky obeyed and took a step back. Her heart was pounding and her mind racing for an idea to escape. If only someone else in the house could hear them, but what would the men do if she screamed again? She shuddered.

"What do we do with them?" The familiar voice spoke.

Edwin and Pearl were pushed along with Becky toward the library desk chair. Their backs were up against the desk and suddenly Becky felt something tickling her apron. She looked to her left where Edwin was standing. He tilted his head and slipped his hand behind her back with a book! Of course! Becky thought. He wants me to hide the journal. She was going to try to slip it on top of the desk, but they would surely find it there. She realized there was not much time because as she was deciding, she heard the men whispering and pointing towards the door. Then, the old man summoned them with a wave. Becky just slipped the journal into her apron pocket- she could only hope that they could not see the lump.

As the bald man stepped forward to grab Pearl, she screamed! Maybe someone would hear her. Becky hoped so, but the men were already taking action. The bald one and Hinistrosa grabbed Edwin while the red headed one grabbed Pearl, and the other oddly familiar one stepped out of the dark shadows of the unlit library and grabbed Becky. When he did, all three gasped. Becky could not believe it but it was true…it was Zachery Perkins, Mr. Kendree's personal servant she had thought was so attractive.

They went out into the courtyard and dragged the children to the stables. Once there, they pushed the children into a carriage and then carefully helped the old man up. The bald man climbed in with the other redheaded one and that was when Becky saw that they both were holding guns. Zachery climbed up to drive the carriage. Becky felt dread as she realized that no one could see into the carriage and no one would stop Zachery since everyone at Kendree Hill knew him.

"Who are you? And why are you kidnapping us?" Becky surprised even herself with the question but could not help it. She sometimes talked too much when she was nervous, and right now she was absolutely frightened.   Edwin's eyes almost popped out and Pearl continued to cry, but Old Hinistrosa laughed and then coughed. "You…have…spunk… (cough)…keep talking and we might do a little more than kidnapping…Eh?" He kept laughing almost to himself.

No one said a word until after the carriage had stopped to switch drivers. Zachery came down to sit with them, and the other two men went to sit up in the driver's seat. Perhaps, they were trying to throw off witnesses? Becky could not be sure. Soon after the stop, Old Hinistrosa fell asleep. It was now dark and the carriage kept rattling along. Gradually, Pearl and Edwin fell asleep too, but Becky kept her eyes wide open. It was now the break of dawn. They had ridden all through the night. She couldn't see anything, for they had drawn heavy shutters over the windows, so she did not know where she was; however, she thought that they had come into a town for she could feel the bumps of cobbled streets. Her mind wandered to her brothers and sisters. What were her twin brothers doing on the sea? How was Susannah? Was she doing well in the factory? She wished she were there to help her. And how were her little brother and sisters doing with Aunt Matilda? Were they afraid of her still, or was she treating them more kindly? At that moment, Becky wished that she was with them- she would rather suffer Aunt Matilda than be in this carriage. She started to sniff back tears welling up in her gray eyes which only resulted in her whole body shaking.

"Stop crying, Becky," Zachery spoke.

Becky stopped her crying and stiffened her back. She was not going to let him think she was afraid.

"I will not let them harm you," Zachery said and spoke with affection as he patted her shoulder.

Becky's tearful eyes flashed in anger. "Take your hands off of me," she dared to whisper through clenched teeth. "You disgust me!"

Zachery took his hand off of her shoulder, "If it were not for me, Becky, you and your little bratty friends would be dead."

"But why would you even be one of them? They are grotesque! I thought you were…" Becky was interrupted. Becky did not get a reply for as soon as she asked the question, the carriage stopped. Everyone was awakened and piled out. Becky could tell they were in a large city…perhaps London…but where? She glanced around and saw she was in a dark alley.

"We leave from here soon," Zachery whispered.

"Where are we?" She whispered back.

"Billingsgate Port," he said.

She flashed a fearful look at him. If they were at Billingsgate then that meant they were in London. And that meant they might be leaving England. But where to? If they left England, there would be little chance of anyone knowing what became of them.

"You!" the bald man pointed at Becky, "you stay with this carriage. The other two, come with me and Gus now!" He shouted at Edwin and Pearl. Pearl stopped and gave Becky a quick hug and ran after the bald man sobbing. Edwin was a little reluctant to leave.

"Goodbye, Becky Blake. If we…if we never see each other again …I want you to know that all of those ugly words I've called you…well, I take back every mean thing I ever said," Edwin said slowly and then lowered his voice, "don't let them have it…it has to be the map," he whispered. He spun away from Becky before she could say anything. She watched him run around the side of the carriage towards the others.

"Get back in the carriage, Becky," the gentle voice called out. "We will wait here."

"Where are they taking them?" she asked.

"To be questioned. See what they know. I told them that you wouldn't know anything. I know today was your first day in the secret passage," Zachery replied.

"How?"

"Don't ask too many questions...for your own protection."

"But how could you, Zachery? How could you do this to us? I hate you!" Becky yelled.

"Shut your mouth!" Zachery yelled and Becky calmed down but bit her lip in anger.

"Why did you do it?" she breathed.

"Reasons a child like you would not understand," Zachery coolly replied and then turned away from her.

Becky turned away from him too and prayed, "Help me, Lord. Help Pearl and Edwin. Keep them from harm. I am sorry that I have not talked to you as often as Mummy told me to, but help me. Please help Mr. Kendree and the others find us. Please, I pray. Amen."

Suddenly, a thought popped into her mind. She could leave a trail for Mr. Kendree. She looked around to see what she might throw out the door of the carriage which was still open. Becky thought about the journal, but brushed that aside. The others would notice something like that when they brought Pearl and Edwin back, and that would give away the treasure. But why not? If she gave them what they wanted, maybe they would leave them alone? But then again, Zachery said they were going to kill them earlier…so…if they knew too much…they might kill them still? Oh, what should she do? She then reached into her pocket and threw out her hair comb. She tossed it as hard as she could, trying to get it far enough away from the carriage. But suddenly, there was a splash. She had not realized how close to the port they actually were.

"What was that all about, Becky?" Zachery asked.

"I don't know…I just never liked that comb much. Better off with the fish…" she mumbled her lie terribly.

"Yes, I suppose…" Zachery said in that oddly gentle voice of his. Becky did not know how to read him. "Stay in here! I will be right outside the carriage, so don't try anything," he suddenly ordered.

When he stepped outside, Becky pulled out the journal from her skirts. She flipped through the leather book until she came to a hand drawn picture. She had gone to school until the age of twelve, so she knew the basics of her letters, numbers, and enough to know a little geography. She saw a hand drawn picture of what looked like the Mediterranean Sea. As she was trying to study it, she heard Zachery talking to the others. She decided to tear out the picture of the map and put it in her petticoat. She placed the journal quickly back in her pocket as the carriage door burst open. "I'm sorry, Becky, but it seems Hinistrosa would like to talk to you after all."

CHAPTER EIGHT

Becky was led by Zachery to an alleyway close to the docks. Pearl and Edwin were standing there, and she wondered why they did not run, but as she drew closer, she saw the other men had guns to their backs. She bit her lip as she gazed at Old Hinistrosa. He was tall yet stooped and his pale brown eyes seemed to be laughing at her as she stood before him.

"Ah...so you are the little maid that the young Kendree spoke of," Old Hinistrosa sneered. Becky flashed a fearful look at Edwin, and he hung his head in defeat. Was he worried that she would snitch so easily about the journal? Becky had no intentions to.

"Your employer had to be reasoned with. He and his dear cousin have confessed that they overheard our conversation from the secret passage, and that they do in fact have what we are looking for...Sir Frankford Kendree's journal!" Hinistrosa said and laughed his raucous laugh. He lifted a cigar to his wrinkled mouth. Becky looked over at Edwin again and saw that he was rubbing his hand in disgust. On his hands were cigar burns. She felt so sorry for him and suddenly thought of Pearl but saw with relief that she seemed uninjured.

"Now, then, dear little maid. Where is it?" Old Hinistrosa declared. Becky's gray eyes flashed.

"And will you let us go if I tell you?" she dared to ask.

Old Hinistrosa was not the only one laughing at that. The large red headed man and the bald one chuckled as well.

"You, maybe, but these others will fetch us a good ransom," Hinistrosa said and then added, "I have not yet decided what to do with you- would anyone notice if you just...disappeared?" He coughed out the last word.

Becky shot Zachery a pleading look.

"She has a sister here in London, sir, but she is just a poor factory girl," Zachery said.

"Ahh..." Hinistrosa mused. "Well, then, dear Becky. How about this deal? If you tell me where the journal is, I will let you and your worthless sister live!"

Becky thought of Susannah and at the same time withdrew

the journal. Up to that point, she had thought of running, but if Zachery knew where her sister worked, then the men would find Susannah and harm her. But how did Zachery know she even had a sister? Had he gone through her letters? It seemed with Zachery, anything would be possible to believe now.

Edwin hung his head and let out an exasperated sigh, but Pearl looked a bit relieved as she gave Hinistrosa the journal. Becky was relieved too. The Kendrees would pay the ransom, and they would go home. Hinistrosa could have his ransom and his treasure.

Hinistrosa held the book, "My great grandfather's journal never mentioned the location of Kendree's treasure, but he did mention in it that Sir Kendree wrote faithfully in a journal of his own. At last!" His bony hands skipped through the pages until he came to the last few pages. Becky held her breath. Would he notice the page missing?

He smiled and closed the book. "Make ready to sail!" To her horror, Becky was pulled along by Zachery.

"I thought he was going to set us free!" Becky whispered

through clenched teeth.

"Quiet! Not now, Becky! Hinistrosa would never risk you going back and telling Mr. Kendree. He will wait to send the ransom note when the treasure is safely secured," Zachery whispered back. In broad daylight, they walked along toward a clipper ship with three masts.

The children and the men walked up the ramp slowly, following Hinistrosa's lead. Becky noticed that all hands on the deck seemed to know who he was.

"Senor Hinistrosa," one man, seemingly the captain, said as he bowed.

"Extra pay for you and your men for carrying this special cargo!" Hinistrosa said as he waved flippantly at the children.

"Senor. What cargo?" the bulky captain smirked and waved to two sailors, "send these scamps to the cargo hold!"

"Aye, aye, Captain!" the sailors said in unison. As they were poked with guns by Hinistrosa's men, they had to follow the sailors. Over her shoulder, Becky heard Hinistrosa saying to the captain.

"To Glasgow!" Hinistrosa growled.

Becky swallowed back tears as they were tossed down into the dark cargo hold. Crates were stacked up and there was not much room to even sit. Pearl started to cry again, and Becky put her arm around her shoulder.

"We will be fine. They are just keeping us until they find the treasure, and then you can go home," she said to the girl.

"The treasure is not in Scotland, Becky," Edwin whispered. He ruffled his hair in frustration.

"Then why did Hinistrosa tell the captain to take us there?" Becky asked.

"I have no idea. I read the journal, and it never said the treasure was *in* Scotland...only that he planned to put it there."

"Well, perhaps he did?" Becky said hopefully.

Edwin shook his head, "He is going to our estate near Edinburgh, I bet. But, it's funny, why would he take us where someone would know us? My father will come and teach him a lesson," Edwin said in what he meant to be a brave tone, but it came out as he truly felt- scared.

"Who knows…Perhaps, Hinistrosa will hide us somewhere other than your property," Becky suggested. "The best we can do now is keep our heads. There is nowhere to run on a ship."

Pearl grabbed her stomach in between her tears, "I am not feeling so well. I will probably get sick at first…I did on the way here from Savannah…"

Becky sat down on the floor and patted her back. Being at sea was like a second home to her, she had gone out with her father on his fishing boat on several occasions. She sat down, "If only we had a bit of ginger for you…" she mused aloud. Ginger naturally calmed the stomach, but she doubted that there was any on board.

"What is this cargo, anyway?" Becky asked. Pearl was still lying on the floor moaning with seasickness, so Edwin and Becky decided to snoop around and see if they could find anything to help the girl.

They were peeking around and saw that one of the crates

actually looked like it was half open. Becky reached to open it all the way and when she lifted the coarse wooden lid, she let out a scream! Out popped a little, dirty girl of about seven or eight. She had mousy brown tangled hair and tattered beggar clothes.

"Oye, this is my hiding spot, then! Get your own!" The little girl screeched.

"I…I am sorry…Well what are you doing here?" Becky gasped. She could not believe her eyes.

By then, Edwin and Pearl gathered around the girl in the crate. The little girl was standing on bundles of cloth and lace and a held a cracker in one hand and a large jug of water in the other.

"Who are you!" Edwin demanded. He used his authoritative high-brow tone which irritated Becky very much. And it seemed to irritate the little girl too, for she said,

"Me name is Loopie! Loopie Robins!" the girl squeaked and then added, "And who the blazes are you?"

CHAPTER NINE

Loopie Robins, the waif of a little girl flashed her eyes back and forth at them like a cornered cat. Becky said to her softly, "It's alright, we won't hurt you."

"Aye, but I may hurt you!" Loopie snapped at her.

"Easy now, little girl!" Edwin said in his patronizing tone of his.

"She's alright, Edwin. She's just frightened," Becky countered him with her own strict voice.

"I am not scared. You just stole my hiding place is all!" Loopie said again, but there was a bit of a quiver in her lip this time.

"We are terribly sorry…You see…we were kidnapped and had no choice," Becky said. "Why are you hiding down here, anyways?"

"I think I am going to be sick!" Pearl groaned and clutched her stomach.

"Well, I'm just trying to get away from that terrible place! I wasn't going to stay there another minute. I had to get out, I did!"

Loopie sniffed then, and Becky could tell she was sniffing back tears.

"What place?" Becky said gently.

"The workhouse...they split me up from my family..."

Loopie said.

"Well, you should not have run away for that reason!" Edwin

interjected, "Workhouses are fine establishments for people who

cannot find work and manage on their own."

Becky glared at him and then turned to Loopie and put her

arm around the frail girl. "I am so sorry. You must miss your family

terribly. But running away will not help. What do you plan to do

when we land?"

"I can manage," Loopie said but her voice was far from being

confident. Becky felt so sorry for the girl. She missed her family as

well and knew how it was to be split apart. She got very protective

over the little girl.

"Well, you shouldn't let the man in charge of this boat catch

you," Becky said. "I wish we could help you out when we land, but unfortunately, we are being kidnapped as I told you before. Best we don't tell anyone she is here, right?" Becky directed the question to both Edwin and Pearl, but poor Pearl did not hear her and Edwin just grunted. He obviously did not know what to think of the dirty little poor girl. Becky wondered if he had ever really taken a good look at a poor person before. Probably not.

"Well…I could help you hide too!" Loopie said suddenly. She seemed to have let down her guard after Becky had hugged her.

"I am sure they would find us in the crate. They surely would know," Becky said.

"Well, now, Becky, we could at least try…" Edwin said.

"But then we would give Loopie away," Becky whispered as she stepped away from Loopie and pulled Edwin to the side.

Edwin shrugged her arm off of him. "Well, we could hide in different crates. Do you really think she is better off just becoming a street child in Glasgow?" Edwin said quickly. Pearl moaned from her corner.

"I agree…what do we have to lose? They won't do anything

to that girl- she doesn't know anything, and it is obvious no one could pay any kind of ransom. We should at least hide." Pearl said.

Loopie looked at them, "Why did they kidnap you?" she said and nibbled on her cracker again.

"We cannot say…" Becky said quickly, "for your protection, I mean. We should not tell you anything."

"Well, I can see why they might capture Mr. Fancy Britches and the sick princess over there for a ransom, but why you? Why you then?" Loopie asked. She was very young but very intelligent Becky thought.

"It is a big mess, "Becky said to her. They heard footsteps above them. "Best get back in your crate, Loopie. But first, would you mind terribly, if my sick friend has a couple of your crackers- to ease her stomach?" Becky asked.

"Well…I suppose so…but only a couple!" Loopie sat back down in her crate and grabbed two crackers and handed them to Becky.

"Thank you, Loopie," Becky said and walked over to Pearl.

"Here, eat these. Then your stomach will at least have something in it."

Pearl groaned and just nodded as she took the crackers.

Edwin was already opening three other crates. "Here, Pearl, get in here." He pointed at one to the left of Loopie's. Pearl stood up, grabbing her stomach with one hand and holding the crackers with her other hand. "I hope this works, but if not at least it is comfier than sitting on the wooden floor," she said. She slowly climbed into the crate and lay down on the bundles of lace. They helped her put the lid back over her. The cracks in the boards of the wood were enough for breathing. Loopie really had found a nice hiding place for a stowaway. Of course, Hinistrosa having a lace merchant ship helped too.

Edwin motioned for Becky to get into another crate beside Pearl's. "Edwin," Becky whispered, "Before I get in, I need to show you something that I kept from Sir Frankford's journal." Becky pulled out the map.

"The Mediterranean," Edwin exclaimed and then covered his

mouth as he had spoken very loudly.

Becky nodded, "I thought so. And look…there are some funny pictures on it but no legend!" Becky showed him the map.

There was an elaborate picture of a rock at the bottom of Spain and a gate at the opening from the Atlantic Ocean to the Mediterranean Sea. A tiny embossed cross at the top of the rock stood out on the page almost like a compass rose.

"What do you think of it? Is this where the treasure is?" Becky asked. She had not gotten a chance to really look at it before because Zachery had shown up so quickly back at the carriage.

"Yes, of course!" Edwin was really excited now. He rubbed his hand through his thick blonde hair, "Spain! But don't you see. If we are going to Glasgow, then the rest of the journal must be leading Hinistrosa somewhere else. I can't believe that I didn't see this before. I thought I had read the entire book, but somehow I missed studying this page. At the end of the journal, he said that he wanted to take his treasure to his estate. But why would he draw this map pointing to Spain?"

"Perhaps...look...Edwin...there is writing on the back of the map," Becky dared to breathe.

Edwin turned the map over. In fancy lettering there was an odd little poem of which he read aloud.

The key to the treasure awaits

Lying at the old sea's gate.

Find it near the majestic rock

Where only the holy dare to knock.

"What does it mean?" Becky asked.

"The Rock of Gibraltar!" Edwin whispered. And he looked at her and his eyes danced. "Sir Frankford Kendree fought with the Anglo Dutch and helped claim Gibraltar for the English. He supposedly had Hinistrosa's great great whatever help him. He must have hidden the treasure at the Rock!"

"But what does only the holy mean?" Becky asked. She had heard of the Rock of Gibraltar but didn't think there was anything holy about it.

"That I don't know…but plan on finding out. I want to get this treasure before they do. When we land…we need to find a way to escape. And then, I want to get on a ship to Gibraltar!" Edwin declared and then looked at her shocked face.

"No, Edwin, if we escape, we need to go home to your parents," Becky said but another part of her wanted a sea adventure too.

"With my knowledge of the journal, and your knowledge of sailing, we could do it! We could find the treasure for ourselves before they do! If you help me, Becky, I will give you a fair share of the treasure! If we don't do it, they will surely figure it out and then we would have nothing. So, you see, if we run… We need to run to the treasure!" Edwin said and then grinned at her. He seemed like he had just won a college scholarly debate or something.

"But if I run, Hinistrosa said he would hurt my sister…" Becky added.

Pearl, who had been eavesdropping on their conversation, interjected, "I could go back to London and warn your sister and go on to tell Uncle what is going on. As much as I love adventure, this seasickness is not for me. So you see, Becky, just tell me where your sister is and you needn't worry. I'll run back to London while you two get the treasure. I'll warn your sister and then go to Kendree Hill. Meanwhile, you should be able to get to Gibraltar and the treasure. Just make sure you get to it first."

Becky looked at Pearl and then back at Edwin. If Pearl could warn Susannah, then nothing was stopping her from going with Edwin, and if he was true to his word and gave her some of the treasure, then she could possibly get her family back together. She bit her lip and finally said, "Well, Edwin, find me a boat, and we'll find you some treasure," And as she said it, she smiled. She thought of her father just then. She would have to draw on everything he had taught her about the sea. It was dangerous and crazy, but somehow, she knew she could do it. She had her mother's determination and her father's love of the sea- a perfect combination for whatever danger lay ahead.

CHAPTER TEN

Sir Frankford Kendree hovered over Becky in her dreams that night. His arms were folded as he leaned up against the wall. The man's face was the same as in the painting, yet this time, in her dream, he was smiling a wide smile and nodding his head slowly up and down. He placed his hands out in front of him and kneeled down as if to pray. Suddenly, Becky woke up sweaty, heart racing and jumped up, bumping her head against the hard lid of the crate. It took her several moments to remember why she was in the belly of a ship.

"Are you alright?" Pearl voiced in a whisper from her crate.

"Yes…just a bad dream," Becky whispered back. She really didn't think that this would work. She got out of the crate and tried to guess how far it would take to get to Glasgow. It should not be much longer. She went over to Pearl's crate and continued the conversation, "We should come up with a plan about how to get you back to London without them noticing. We might be reaching Glasgow soon."

"What is wrong with you out there, Becky? Go back to sleep!" Edwin interjected from his crate.

Becky bit her tongue, so as not to wake up the rest of the ship. Oh, that boy! She went over and knocked on his crate, "This is not a holiday, Edwin. We need to plan. We need to act before they reach port." She whispered through her teeth. How could she explain to Edwin, that her intuition usually was correct, and she was feeling very uneasy about their hiding place, considering they had found Loopie so easily.

"Simple…" Becky heard the squeaky Cockney voice of Loopie. "We don't wait 'til the boat stops for them to discover us," Loopie said as she too, got out of her crate. "Everybody knows you got to keep finding hiding spots to never get caught. Aye, I know how to keep one step ahead of them, I does." The frail girl nodded her head firmly and placed her hands on her hips.

By this time, all four children were out of the crates and standing. Pearl, looking rather green, yet a little better than the day before spoke to Loopie, "So where do you suggest we go now?"

Loopie shrugged, "Well, I could go and sneak around a bit…I thinks I'm the only one that's any good at sneaking, anyways."

Becky felt suddenly very protective of the little girl. Suppose they caught her? What would they do, "You shouldn't go alone…"

Loopie laughed, "I'd rather be on me own than have any big goofy kids giving me away. I can dodge a crowd, if you know what I mean."

"I do know what you mean!" Edwin said through clenched teeth, disdain on his face, "You are nothing but a filthy little thief. That's what!"

"Edwin," Becky said, glaring at him.

"What if I is, and what if I ain't?" Loopie retorted back at Edwin.

This time, Becky saw Pearl walk over to Edwin to hold him back from charging the girl.

"Calm down, now, Edwin. She's helping us. What does it matter what she is?" Pearl said.

"Well, I still have morals! And I say we don't get any more help from the likes of her," Edwin said.

At that moment, Becky, even though she was Edwin's servant, wanted to box his ears but instead, said, "Edwin, we have no choice. We have to trust her," Becky then leaned closer to Pearl and Edwin, "And I don't think this little street girl had much choice in her life. Do you even know how terrible workhouses really are? Do not judge her for her past…give her a chance to prove herself. After all, she may be our only hope of getting out of here."

Edwin still looked furious; however, he softened a little. And he slowly nodded his approval without, for once, saying anything.

"Right then," Loopie smiled. "Be back as I go up me apples and pears!"

"What?" Pearl asked, totally confused. But the girl took off up the cargo stairs.

"Pearl, you will remember the address where my sister is?" Becky asked. She was worried about what Zachery had said about her sister. He must have read the outside address from her sister's letters. She still could not believe that Zachery was involved in all of this. And she suspected that Julie was too. Why else would the sourly maid have told them to meet Master Kendree in the library? Who else in the house had been in on it, she wondered. Her thoughts then turned to the present situation, and she suddenly wondered how Edwin planned on getting to Gibraltar with no money.

"Edwin, how do you plan on getting a boat?" Becky asked.

Edwin looked down and pulled out a small brass pocket watch. "I plan on finding a pawn shop to get some money for a boat."

"But, Edwin, that will not be enough for a boat!" Becky protested. She should have discussed this before going to sleep last night.

"Well, how the blazes should I know!" Edwin responded, very irritated.

"Shhh….quiet." Pearl reminded them.

Becky put her hand to her forehead and shrugged her

shoulders. "I am sorry. I just thought you had a plan."

"I do. Go to Gibraltar. Find the treasure," Edwin tried to sound brave, but his voice fell a little flat.

"Edwin," Pearl whispered, "What if you went to your Edinburgh estate? I mean if we can sneak off of here, you could go there before Hinistrosa. He will be left looking for us, not knowing we are one step ahead of him," Pearl, despite her sick complexion, looked quite pretty again as her eyes sparkled with excitement at her newfound plan.

"But that is crazy!" Becky protested. "Why should we go where Hinistrosa is ultimately headed?"

"Listen to me," Pearl said and suddenly grimaced. When she had recovered a little, she continued. "Edwin, you must know where uncle keeps some money at the estate. You also will have some time ahead of Hinistrosa because he will be looking for us in Glasgow or back in London."

Edwin was nodding with excitement. "Yes! Of course, I know where he keeps some of his money. There is a secret drawer in his study!" So, Edwin, very readily took to the idea of going to Edinburgh. He and Pearl stood grinning with excitement to see Becky's reaction.

Becky thought it over. Part of her thought this adventure truly exciting yet part of her found it too daring…and yes…even a little addled. But in the end, her adventurous side took over as well as that thought again of what she could do with her share of the treasure. "Yes, as long as we get there before anyone can find us. And as long as Pearl goes back to London and Kendree Hill…"

At the moment of her agreement, Loopie popped out of the cargo stairs. "Well, we can hide under the lifeboats. They be so close, that when we dock, we can easily slip down the gangplank!"

Becky patted the girl on the back, "Wonderful job, Loopie."

"Did anyone see you?" Edwin asked sternly.

Loopie shook her head no.

"Well, we best get going, then!" Loopie said. "Follow me!"

Edwin, Pearl, and Becky all looked at each other to see what the others were going to do.

"Well, I for one am getting out of here," Pearl said and followed Loopie.

"Me too!" Edwin said, "Coming, Becky?"

"Yes," she looked back at the cargo hold and followed them up the dark stairs. As she climbed, she silently prayed that all would go well- for there was so much that could go wrong.

CHAPTER ELEVEN

As planned, the four children crept stealthily off the boat and onto the Glasgow docks. Loopie led the way. Dawn had broken through the night, and as Becky glanced at the light coming up in brilliant pink rays, she also seemed to find a dawning of peace come to her as they made their escape from the ship that had held them captive.

"Well, we made it off the boat, now how do we pay for passage on another?" Pearl said suddenly. She was trying to fix her blonde curls with a fancy emerald hair comb.

"Pay? Don't need to pay, miss," Loopie said. "Leave that to me. We can hop right back on another boat as soon as we figure out which one is headed back to London."

"I say! Pearl, we can't have you getting caught as a stowaway. We surely could pawn something to get you safe passage. We are Kendrees, after all, not criminals!" Edwin said rather smugly.

Loopie stood there with her hands still on her hips. "Suit yourself, Fancy Britches, but I can get us home. I can."

Becky nodded, "I think she is right. The sooner we split up, the better. Hinistrosa's men will be looking for three children very soon. And besides, Edwin, we need to use whatever money we get to buy a train ticket to Edinburgh in order to be one step ahead of them."

"But what can we pawn, anyway, Edwin?" Pearl asked, still combing her hair.

Edwin reached out and grabbed her comb.

"Ouch! What was that for?" Pearl said. She was about to grab it back before she figured it out. He wanted her emerald comb in addition to his brass watch to book them train tickets.

"I see…but it was so very pretty," Pearl said longingly looking at her precious comb.

"Well, we best be hiding. Quick, we need to find a ship back," Loopie said and tugged on Pearl's sleeve.

"Yes, you must. Be safe, both of you," Becky said as she hugged Pearl, "Goodbye…and promise to warn my sister before going to Kendree Hill."

"Yes of course, Becky," Pearl promised.

"And you," Becky squeezed Loopie. "You clever girl, be careful…and do try to catch back up with your family. Family is what keeps us going when times such as these get harsh! Never forget that!" Loopie looked up at her with sad little knowing eyes as she nodded her head.

"Thank you, Becky. For being kind to me…." Loopie said and wiped a stray tear from her face. But just as soon as the little girl was almost overcome with emotion, she composed herself. Becky thought again how very old the little girl seemed for her age.

"Well, dear cousin, be careful! When we meet again, we will have treasure beyond your imagination!" Edwin clapped Pearl on the back.

"Goodbye," Pearl whispered to them both.

"Goodbye!" Edwin and Becky both exclaimed.

Becky stood watching Loopie and Pearl dart along the wharf in search of a London bound ship.

"Well, maid, it is just up to us to beat Hinistrosa at his own game!" Edwin said. He slipped the emerald comb in one of his pockets and patted his pocket watch with his other hand.

"Yes, Edwin. We better ask someone to help us get to the train station."

"Yes! Good thinking. Come along then." Edwin said.

They walked a few blocks away from the docks. The place seemed suddenly alive with fisherman and sailors milling about. Becky closed her eyes and breathed in the familiar smell of the sea. The salt air mixed with fish lingered on her nostrils. The seabirds called to her. She stopped, forgetting their mission, and took it all in. With her eyes still closed, a trace of a smile broke out onto her face.

"Good morning, lass!" a young boy's voice broke into her thoughts.

Startled, Becky looked up into a pair of smiling royal blue eyes. She shielded her hand from the sun to see the rest of the boy. A boy with a shock of red curly hair leaned against a pole, flexing his strong, wiry muscles while tying a knot on a piece of rope.

"Yes, it is!" Becky said. She returned his smile.

"Aye. Tis. So, what is such a bonnie girl such as yourself doing out here so early?" the boy asked.

With his simple question, Becky got suddenly nervous. She should not be talking to this boy. He could be questioned later by Hinistrosa's men, and she did not want to get caught nor did she want the boy to get hurt.

"My name is Charlie McCoy. What's yours?" the boy asked but before she could answer him, she heard Edwin call for her.

"Becky! Hurry up!"

Charlie McCoy's eyes danced when he heard Edwin shriek, "I would not want to keep you waiting from your *gentleman*." He tugged hard on a knot he was working on.

"He's not..." Becky started but quickly stopped herself. She was talking too much.

"Good day then, Becky," Charlie said.

"Good day." Becky smiled and turned quickly, still looking at the boy named Charlie, when she suddenly smacked right into Edwin.

"Becky, whatever are you doing!" Edwin snapped. "What kind of time is it to take a break? We have to get going, you silly maid!"

"I was talking to this *gentleman*, here," Becky sarcastically said as she glared at Edwin. She knew that using the word gentleman on a fisherman was sure to make his blood boil, but she didn't care.

Charlie McCoy laughed delightfully. "We were just talking about the beautiful day, sir. Never you mind. It was not your maid's fault. She was trying to leave, but I kept asking questions." Becky stared over at the boy and could not get over how huge his smile was.

His kindness seemed to irk Edwin even more, "Very well, but we are trying to find a train station. Could you be a good boy and tell us where it is?"

Charlie did not drop his smile but his eyes narrowed at the word boy. "Yes sir, I can give you directions." Charlie proceeded to tell them the quickest way to find the station.

Becky nervously shifted her weight and tugged on Edwin's sleeve as Charlie finished giving the directions. She was upset that Edwin had asked him instead of someone closer to the town. Hinistrosa was bound to ask around the docks. She also wanted to get the two boys away from each other before Edwin got himself completely whipped by Charlie.

"Let's go. Quickly," she said. She turned to Charlie McCoy, "Thank you, and please…do not tell anyone you saw us….they may ask."

Charlie McCoy's smile wiped away from his face in an instant and was replaced with concern, "Are you alright, miss? Say the word, and I will help you."

"I am fine…it's just…I can't say. But thank you," Becky looked up at him and managed a weak smile.

Although not convinced, Charlie McCoy tipped his hat, "You have my word, Becky."

They looked at each other another very long second which

caused Becky to blush. "Thank you," she finally whispered.

"Yes, thank you," Edwin said as he and Becky hurried away. As she walked away, Becky could not help but think of her first meeting with Charlie McCoy...for she sensed it would not be her last.

CHAPTER TWELVE

On their way to the train station, Becky and Edwin found a small pawn shop just opening for business. They quickly received money for the comb and pocket watch; however, Becky felt they deserved more than they received. Still, it was enough for tickets to Edinburgh on the next train and there was still a lot to spare. In fact, while waiting, Becky bought a scarf to wrap around her uniform. She also threw her apron away. It would not do to have Hinistrosa asking after a maid and still look the part.

Their train, thankfully, was leaving within the hour, so all was well with their plan. They should arrive before Hinistrosa and his men discovered that they had not all gone back to London. All was well, except for the fact that the plan was so risky. Becky could not believe that they were going where Hinistrosa would soon follow. When she and Edwin boarded the train, Edwin held both of their tickets out to the ticketmaster who stared awhile before taking them. His eyebrows raised, "Traveling alone...just the two of you?"

"Of course," Edwin said with confidence, "We always travel in the summer to visit our dear grandmother." The man smiled at that and waved them on. Becky's heart beat a bit and she lowered her head down even more as she boarded...she did not want them to be suspicious of her.

"It would help if you weren't wearing that disgusting frock!" Edwin whispered through his teeth.

"What am I to do?" Becky asked. She agreed though. She hardly looked related to Edwin dressed in her tattered uniform and cheap shawl.

As they moved inside to their seats, the train started moving. With each mile, Becky started to relax, though not enough to actually fall asleep like Edwin who soon was snoring loudly. Instead, she enjoyed the Scottish countryside passing by. She loved the green and the blur of wildflowers of blue and purple. The trip was to take about three and a half hours, so Becky had plenty of time to think. And as she thought, she realized how crazy their plan really was. Her stomach began to turn in knots as she thought of getting caught by Hinistrosa's men again. Perhaps, once there, they could get a message to Master Kendree. A butler, maybe, who could send a telegraph? Yes, as she thought of it, she relaxed a little. Why did she think she was going to actually go through risking her life all for the sake of money anyways? She rubbed her forehead as she thought. If only her mother or father had been there to talk some sense into her earlier. Then she would have been on her way back to London with the other girls and closer to safety. Well, at least her mother would have talked sense, but her father probably would have jumped onto a ship to Gibraltar already. She smiled at the thought of her father. Aunt Matilda was not altogether right…she was not just like her father: he was brave and adventurous, and here she was being afraid. Still, even with the hope of getting part of the treasure and getting her family back together, was it worth risking her life? She did not think so…or did she? She struggled with this the entire ride, and as the train moved swiftly, she caught site of wild thistle growing stubbornly out of rocks. She grinned. Hope sometimes blooms most brilliantly in the most unlikely and harshest of places.

Once in Edinburgh, Edwin knew his way around. He even knew where to find two horses from a stable to ride to the Kendree's northern estate: Blairwick Manor. "It is only a few miles from town," Edwin said as he mounted a white horse. Becky needed a little boost to get on her black and white speckled horse, but once on, she felt steadier. She was not used to riding, but hoped Edwin could not tell; however, he knew immediately.

"Well, you should have told me you could not ride!" Edwin said shaking his head.

"I did not know this was part of your *master plan!*" Becky retorted as the horse moved unsteadily underneath her.

"Should we just walk? Or do you think you can ride?" Edwin asked. "We do not have time for me to give you a lesson after all!" He shook his head side to side.

"Give me time…I can manage…" Becky patted the horse on the neck, "Right girl?" she soothed in the horse's ear.

"Thank goodness it is not too far…there is probably no need to hurry, so we will just take it slow. Come, I will ride beside you to help," he said and taught her briefly a way to hold the reigns more tightly and taught her a few commands as well. Soon, Becky had graduated from a very slow gait to a slow trot. Instead of feeling fear, she began to gain confidence. She smiled over at Edwin.

"Thank you," she said.

"For what," he asked, startled. He knitted his eyebrows in confusion.

"For teaching me to ride. For this adventure," Becky said.

He stared at her sideways, and almost returned her smile but instead looked forward and cleared his throat, "It will not be an adventure if we do not stick to the plan."

Evidently, his plan still did not include talking on equal terms to a maid, Becky thought. Same old Edwin: selfish as ever. She did not know why it upset her so much. After all, they were from very different and distinct classes, but still, she wished he would treat her with more respect.

They came off the road and onto a smaller off beaten path. Wildflowers were everywhere now. There were yellow lady's bedstraw, purple heather, and even blue thistle.

"We are almost there," Edwin excitedly exclaimed. He looked again at her sideways as they came to a clearing around a bend in the path. Becky caught her breath, for although the house was not nearly as huge as Kendree Hill, to her, it was more beautiful. Light gray stone walls topped with a darker slated roof. Climbing lavender and wild pink roses spread upwards on the stone walls. It was almost magical to her. She felt as if she believed in fairies again as they neared it.

"It is beautiful," she whispered.

"Yes, it is! It is my father's favorite place. I believe your mother worked there as a girl?" Edwin asked and had a slight derogatory tone in his voice as he talked of her mother.

"Yes, I believe so," Becky said, ignoring Edwin's tone for once. Her mother had actually been in this magical place before her. Blairwick Manor, with its wild beauty, almost made Becky forget the possible danger that lay ahead.

CHAPTER THIRTEEN

They put the horses in the stable and walked to the oak door of the stone house. Birds chirped in the air as they banged the large knocker back and forth. An old man answered. He had a thin, lanky figure.

"Mr. Jeffries," Edwin said very calmly and with authority.

"Why, Young Master Edwin! I did not receive word of your visit! Come in, sir, come in!"

Becky and Edwin walked inside the house. They stepped into a blue gray foyer. The old man looked questionably at Becky. Becky nudged Edwin.

"This is Becky, our newest maid, Mr. Jeffries. Mother sent her to clean the silver and pack it for her as she is an expert in such," Edwin said. Becky rolled her eyes. That was all he could come up with?

Mr. Jeffries still looked a bit unsure but nodded, "Of course, Master Edwin. Is your mother preparing for a visit to Blairwick soon? "

"Yes…I mean…not for another month or two. It is just… she just wanted them for a party at Kendree Hill…"

"I see. Well, my dear girl, you may find the silver in a box shut up in storage in the dining room at the moment. I am afraid we only have a part time maid that comes once a week when the Kendrees are away. I am the only one that stays full time, you see."

"And Mr. Jeffries…would you mind terribly uncovering some of the furniture in the library? I would like to read while I wait for the maid."

"Yes, sir, and which room will you be staying in?" Mr. Jeffries asked.

"Staying? Oh, we are not staying the night. We just came for the silver, and then we will head back to our train."

Mr. Jeffries looked sharply at him. Why oh why did he make up the silver? And why did Becky even come inside? She realized now, she should have stayed and waited for him in the stable. But all the man said was, "Yes of course, sir. I will just prepare the library for you then. Well, my dear lass, the dining room is the second door on the left." The old man managed a smile and rather slowly walked to what she supposed was the library.

"What was the silver all about?" Becky said.

"I don't know. It does not look proper...us traveling together. He is sure to contact father and mother as soon as we leave. We can't stay long. Grab the silver, so Mr. Jeffries does not think anything of it and then meet me in the library. I will get some of the money out of my father's desk and leave him a note as well. Hurry, we don't know if Hinistrosa found out we were on a train headed here or on a boat headed back to London."

Becky nodded her head. She walked quickly over to the dining room. Why not just tell Mr. Jeffries the truth and head back to London? She could not help thinking of it. It would be so simple and so safe...yet if she followed through and helped Edwin find his treasure, she could do so much with her share of the money. She could maybe get her family back together and the younger ones away from Aunt Matilda. And that was worth the chance. She pondered this as she stepped into the beautiful dining room. It was painted a robin's egg blue. Rich dark furniture adorned the room. She headed over to the side table where she supposed the silver was. She opened it gingerly. The silver was in need of a good polishing; however, she did not plan on doing that then. She snapped the lid shut and headed back towards the room where she had seen Mr. Jeffries go earlier.

She stepped into the dark green library only to be yelled at by Edwin. "You should have announced you were coming!" He was shoving a pull out drawer back into a desk which when closed appeared to not even exist.

"Why? It is not like we are formal now that we are in on this crazy venture anyways? Why should I announce every time I enter a room?"

Edwin looked up, rather frustrated. "Because...because it is the thing to do!"

"Edwin, I would not tell anyone about that secret compartment. Would not you know that by now? Why not just trust me?"

"I suppose I reacted a bit rashly. I apologize, Becky. I just did not want anyone to see my father's desk. I feel a tad guilty going in it myself, you see," Edwin replied. He seemed to be a bit nervous.

"Well, I have the money. It is enough. And I left a note for father not to worry. I explained we were looking for the treasure but did not put where as I was afraid Hinistrosa's men might find it."

"A good idea," Becky said.

"Well, I did not want them to think…to think I had run away for other reasons."

Becky blushed. Is that why Mr. Jeffries had looked at her so funny? Did he think that she and Edwin had run away together? Why they were too young for that sort of thing! Honestly! At least if all is well, Pearl should be able to tell the Kendrees everything soon.

"I thought you could help me look for some books on the treasure or on Gibraltar, but we need to be quick!"

"Of course," Becky said. She looked at the rows and rows of books on the shelves. They would have a lot to go through. "I'll start with the shelf on the left."

"Very good. I'll take the one on the right."

Becky climbed up the library ladder and started to thumb

through the first couple of books. What a lovely house this was! If they were not in such a hurry, she would love to explore more of the books. But instead, she settled for reading the book spines. The first several were botany books. She really could not help opening the *History of Botany.*

"Hurry, Becky! We do not have all day!" Edwin snapped, so she closed the book and returned it carefully to its place.

"Sorry. These are all botany books over here. What do you have over there?"

"Silly stuff. Fiction, you know! I think we should try the middle shelf."

"Sounds like a plan," Becky said and as she tried to step down, she leaned too far to the right which sent the ladder swaying with her.

"Careful, Becky. I say…just break up the place!" Edwin came to steady the ladder and help her down.

Once she was down, she looked at the middle shelf. This would be the section. There were a lot of old history and geography books. They looked through the titles when Becky stumbled upon one:

History of Gibraltar.

"Edwin! I found one!"

Edwin got excited and grabbed it from her. He was turning pages and studying a map.

Becky felt a chill run through her spine and suddenly shivered.

"Edwin, please, let's grab it and go. I have a funny feeling...I can't explain it."

"Oh but please do explain!" Another voice answered her. Edwin and Becky turned their heads quickly in its direction.

Standing before them was Zachery Perkins.

"Zachery!" Becky exclaimed and her eyes flashed with anger. She still could not believe he was a part of Hinistrosa's men.

"Dear Becky," Zachery said very smoothly. He stepped towards her, so she stepped towards Edwin.

"Stop where you are, Zachery," Edwin tried to say with authority, yet his voice cracked.

Zachery smiled, "Or what? You might be the master in your head, but to me you are just a boy!"

"Mr. Jeffries!" Edwin yelled.

"Don't bother calling that old man."

"What did you do him?" Becky asked...her stomach getting in knots.

"Don't worry, Becky. I haven't done that. I only locked the old man in the cupboard under the stairs," Zachery laughed again at her fear. He turned again to Edwin, "Now...what made you come here? Why not go back to daddy?"

"How did you know we were coming here?" Edwin countered.

"Know? Why that is the best part. I didn't. It was always the plan for us to come here, but since all of our hostages went missing, we had to split up. Hinistrosa decided to send me ahead to start looking. I thought the train would be the quickest way here."

"So you are alone?" Edwin asked, his voice getting braver. Becky looked quickly at the boy. He did not possibly think he could

take Zachery did he? She got really worried then. There was no way
Edwin would win. Zachery was right- Edwin was a boy and Zachery
was a full grown man.

"Maybe I am or maybe I am not," Zachery said slowly with an
annoyingly sick grin. "Now, answer my question. Why did you come
here?"

"To beat you to the treasure, naturally," Becky said. Edwin
slapped her in the arm, "Ouch! Well it is true, isn't it?" The fool,
Becky thought. Everyone thought the treasure was here at Blairwick-
no one knew what they knew. "We are looking for the treasure here
at Blairwick."

"Well...I knew Becky had pluck, but Edwin, I must say I am
surprised at your bravery!" He laughed but then suddenly grew
serious. "Well, you should not have come here. In fact, how about a
deal? For Becky's sake of course... I never wanted to get mixed up
in this kidnapping business to begin with. How about you both leave
and go back to Kendree Hill, and I won't breathe a word to
Hinistrosa?"

Becky looked hard at Zachery. She saw the look of sincerity in Zachery's eyes...although there was sadness there too.

"Zachery, do we have your word?" Becky asked. Zachery wiped his sad look away and smiled.

"Good man, then, Zachery. We will do as you say. Promise me, you will not harm old Jeffries. Why not let him go too?" Edwin asked.

"Of course," Zachery said.

"Zachery," Becky said, taking a step towards him. She placed her hand gently on his arm. "Zachery, you have a choice too. You don't have to be one of them," she whispered. He looked at her in surprise. His sad look crept back to his eyes and then changed to anger.

"Leave, before I change my mind! And don't worry about Jeffries. Just go before the others get here!"

"Come on, Becky!" Edwin grabbed her arm and whisked her away from Zachery. It was not until they were outside by the horses that she saw that Edwin had brought the Gibraltar book.

CHAPTER FOURTEEN

After taking the train back to Glasgow, Becky and Edwin headed back to the docks, hoping to acquire a ship and small crew. Once there, however, they discovered that it would be a very difficult if not impossible task. Most of the men they inquired about a ship laughed in their faces, "You, children, need a ship? Ha! Aye, and where are we sailing? To Babyland?"

After so many refusals, Becky was about to give up hope, "Edwin," she said softly, "We could go back to London and tell your father. I am sure he would hire men to go after Hinistrosa and the treasure."

"No!" Edwin said, sitting down on the dock in disgust. "By then, the treasure will be gone. Hinistrosa will have it all for himself!"

"But, Edwin, why do you care so much...I mean...you already have so much money!" Becky said as she knelt down next to him on the rough planks of wood.

He looked up at her furiously, "We have money, that is true, but don't you see. It's not about getting richer, it's about keeping what is rightfully ours! It's about keeping it in the family and not letting someone steal it!"

"But…didn't Sir Frankford steal it in the first place?" Becky asked. "I thought anything taken in military battles belonged to the Crown?"

"Well…I still want to get it for myself and keep it in the family," Edwin said. Becky could not help but think he was just trying to do something to make his father proud of him.

"Your father would be just as proud of you if you went back now…you have acted most bravely!" Becky said. She placed her hand on his arm, but he immediately shook her off.

"You are forgetting your place again!" Edwin retorted.

"Still, we know more about where the treasure is…we could go back now and tell your father. There still could be time to send out a search party before Hinistrosa's," Becky tried to convince him again.

Edwin's shoulders slumped. "Perhaps, you are right. We can just get on a passage back to London and rethink our plan. I did want to find the treasure…not just to uphold my family name but because…because it seemed like such a grand adventure."

"Yes, it did," Becky said. She gazed out longingly to the sea. It had become dusk, and the sun was just setting, streaking the sky with pink and soft yellow.

"Well, look what we have here!" a voice boomed. Becky turned her head and saw a large man leering at her. "I think I found myself another deckhand! How about I Shanghai you, boy, and sell off your sister?" Becky knew from her father what Shanghai mean- it meant taking a person against their will and forcing them to be a sort of slave sailor. Becky looked swiftly around the docks and could not believe this was happening. Of course, it was almost dark, and they were two children alone and vulnerable. Her heart started pounding as she tried to think of what to do. What could they possibly do? She breathed a quick prayer for help.

"Back off, bloke!" she heard a familiar voice say. She glanced and saw with relief, the strong sailor boy, Charlie McCoy.

The boy looked menacing now, staring down the other sailor, his blue eyes piercing and narrowed.

"Slow down, boy. No need to get alarmed…" the large man muttered.

"Pass on by before you regret it," Charlie said. He did not take his eyes off of the man until he did as he said. The man hesitated and then waved his hand.

"Not worth it, boy! Thought they was alone, is all!" The man threw up his arm, waved it, and then passed.

It was not until the man walked away, that Charlie looked down at them. "Well, now, so we meet again, Becky," he smiled broadly at her, "And you, sir…what was your name?"

"Edwin," Edwin mumbled and then added, "Thank you for your help. I had it under control though…"

"Aye, that you did," Charlie chuckled.

"Thank you, Charlie," Becky breathed. Charlie walked over and reached out a hand to help her to her feet.

"Well, then, I thought you had caught a train and left for good,"

Charlie said and squinted down at her. He was a lot taller than she.

"We did," Becky said, "but now we are back."

"I see." Charlie looked questioningly at both of them. "Well, what is your story? Why are you out alone? Did you two run away together?"

"No!" Edwin said furiously. "We are trying to obtain a boat to Gibraltar."

"Gibraltar! Why there?"

"We need to get there to see his grandmother," Becky lied. She did not like lying to someone who possibly had just saved her life, but she did not want him to be questioned by Hinistrosa's men later. The less he knew, the safer he was.

"I cannot figure you two out for the life of me…A young uppity aristocrat and a pretty little maid going to Gibraltar by yourselves? You must admit, it is odd. I think, Edwin was it, I think you promised this lass a bright future and wanted to run off and elope with her! I must say I cannot blame you, but you are both too young as I see it." Charlie crossed his arms and chuckled again.

"Imbecile, we are not eloping. We just need passage to Gibraltar, and I have money to get us there but no one today seems to want my money."

Charlie raised his eyebrows, "Money for passage? Well, my cap'n is not headed to Gibraltar, so you better have enough to change his mind. Come on with me before you get yourselves killed."

Becky and Edwin glanced at each other. Becky wanted to follow Charlie- he had just saved their lives, hadn't he? And besides, she did think they were in more danger staying at the docks come nightfall. "Come on, Edwin. Perhaps he can help," Becky whispered.

Edwin nodded. He and Becky followed Charlie along the docks to a small Yorkshire Billy Boy ship. "Edwin, this is not meant to go off the coast very much," Becky whispered. She knew that the Yorkshire Billy Boy was meant for small traveling off shore and around the inlands. Why, a man and his family could run it. There shouldn't be much of a crew.

She walked over and saw about five sailors and a large red-haired man. "Charlie, my boy! What did you catch today?" The man said and laughed.

"Well, I wanted to throw one back, but the pretty one wouldn't let me," Charlie joked. Edwin grunted in disdain.

"Red, this is Edwin and Becky. Edwin here says he has some money if you want to take him to Gibraltar," Charlie said.

Red looked down at them, "How much money are we talking about, boy?"

"I have this to take us to Gibraltar," Edwin pulled out a stack of money. "And this to get us back," he handed him another, "And this is to keep quiet about it." He placed the last stack in the large man's hand.

The man held it up towards the sky. "Lads, we are changing course. Charlie, introduce your friends to the crew! We sail at dawn!"

CHAPTER FIFTEEN

That night, Becky settled herself down in the ship's one and only cabin. Charlie had very gallantly offered her the cabin. "We can't have you staying in the other quarters now can we?" he had said with a twinkle in his eye. She blushed when he did so for it seemed she had not been treated like a true lady before. Becky wondered if anyone had seen. Edwin had quickly changed topics by demanding to be able to stay in the ship's only cabin instead which is why Charlie had suggested stringing a curtain across.

She settled in and pulled the oil lamp closer up on the makeshift table which was just an overturned barrel. Beside the lamp was the old book of Gibraltar that Edwin had said she could look at. He said earlier that night that he had looked through it but saw no real signs between it and the map they had found in Sir Frankford Kendree's journal.

She opened the book and gingerly leafed through it. Her hand rested on a chapter on St. Michael's Cave. There were some parts that had been named, but the author said that there still were parts that were undiscovered. "I wonder how on earth we are going to find out where it was buried?" she asked herself as she looked at the multiple caves in the Rock of Gibraltar. Becky continued reading, entranced with everything to do with Gibraltar. One cave that caught her eye was named Cathedral Cave. She read that the cave was even thought in ancient times to be one of the Pillars of Hercules, and the caves were thought to be the gateway to Hades, The Underworld. As she read about the mysterious legends, she got a chill and pulled the blanket closer to her. Becky read on about a tragedy that occurred in the caves. Officers of the military often would seek out some adventure by exploring the caverns, and at some point prior to 1840, a Colonel Mitchell in the company of a second officer who wished to explore the caverns interiors were lost, never found nor heard from again. Becky closed the book hurriedly after reading that entry. They would have to figure out a way to keep from getting lost in the cave or else suffer the same fate!

Becky tossed and turned that night, not getting much sleep. When she finally did fall into a deep sleep, dreams of her mother haunted her. Her mother was standing out on a high cliff, overlooking the sea. She turned to her suddenly, fear in her eyes. "Remember to pray, Becky. Remember to pray!" she said over and over again. Becky woke, panting for breath, shaken by how real the dream had seemed. It seemed she could have reached out and touched her dead mother.

"Becky, are you alright in there?" Edwin asked through the curtain. She must have made a scream or sound during her dream.

"Just a bad dream," Becky whispered back.

"Did you find anything new in the book? Any clues?"

"No. Unless…" Becky started, "No never mind."

"What Becky?" Edwin asked.

How could Becky tell Edwin that she still dreamed of her parents and sometimes really still tried to listen to them in her dreams?

"Nothing to tell, really. Just, you remember the poem from the journal? It starts…

The key to the treasure awaits lying at the old sea's gate.

"What was the last line?"

"I believe it was *Find it near the majestic rock where only the holy dare to knock.*" Edwin said.

Her mother had told her to pray over and over again. Could her mother have been sending her the clue they needed to solve the poem's riddle? Gibraltar was the gateway to the Mediterranean Sea thus the line *the key to the treasure awaits lying at the old sea's gate.* Could it be her mother was trying to tell her to pray because she wanted her to know the answer to the next line? *Find it near the majestic rock where only the holy dare to knock.* "The Rock of Gibraltar is the majestic rock and Cathedral Cave is where only the holy knock!" Becky wondered aloud, putting the pieces together.

"Brilliant, Becky!" Edwin said rather loudly for the time of night. "I don't know why I didn't think of it!"

"Yes, well it still is only a guess," Becky said although she smiled at the thought of solving the riddle of the poem. That put them way ahead of Hinistrosa.

"A good guess though! Well, Becky, I suppose I

should get some more sleep," Edwin said, and she even heard

him yawn rather loudly.

"Me too. Goodnight, Edwin," Becky whispered.

"Goodnight, Becky Blake," Edwin said as quietly as he could.

Becky leaned back on her pillow and closed her eyes.

The gentle waves rocked her soothingly to sleep.

The next morning, Becky woke early, for she felt the boat

slowly gaining speed. She opened the curtain separating the cabin

and sneaked past Edwin who was still fast asleep. He was curled up

in a ball with his shoes still on.

Becky climbed up onto the deck to hear shouts from

Red. She caught sight of Charlie McCoy in action, he had on a white

sailor shirt and cap but even through the shirt, she could see his

muscular frame. The older boy waved at her and she saw his grin

spread from ear to ear. She waved shyly back at him. She felt all

nervous all of the sudden, almost like she used to with…with

Zachery. Oh, Zachery! How she had been wrong about him, was

she wrong about Charlie too? She pushed the thought out of her mind. Charlie was nothing like him.

"Good day, lass!" Charlie called. He took his cap off for a second as he acknowledged her, treating her ever as a lady. Becky laughed aloud and smiled back.

"Keep your head in your job, Charlie," one of the other sailors shouted.

"Aye, keep that girl out of the way!" Red called,

"Women bring bad luck to a ship you know, and we wouldn't want her messing with The Seahawk!"

Becky flashed her eyes at Red, "Don't worry about me! I know my way around a boat!"

"You do?" Red laughed, "Well then, my lass, tie me a figure eight knot and let's see!" Red tossed her a bit of rope. Becky, every bit capable thanks to her father and brothers, easily tied it while everyone stopped to watch.

The sailors all laughed and cheered. Charlie swung over to her as he shifted one of the sails. "Well done, Becky!"

"Well, my father was a fisherman," she said proudly.

"Where about?" Charlie said. His eyebrows lifted in surprise, and his blue eyes twinkled.

"Mevagissey,"

"A good fishing port. Is that home too?"

"No. My parents are both...gone now," Becky said. As she said it she noticed that Charlie's pleasant face changed suddenly to that of concern.

"I am sorry," he said softly.

"Charlie! Back to work!" Red bellowed.

"I best get back now, but we will talk later!" Charlie said and then flashed her a dashing smile.

Becky nodded and smiled back at him. She had to

keep herself busy somehow, but it did not seem that Red needed or wanted her help. She decided to go back down in the cabin and wake up Edwin. Perhaps they could get a plan together for exploring Cathedral Cave. As she returned, however, she did not notice that Edwin had already followed her and was standing right behind her.

"Good morning," Becky said.

"Good morning, Becky. Busy?" Edwin's tone was sour and sarcastic.

"Woke up in a bad mood again?" Becky asked.

"No. Just tired of seeing you flirt with everyone. I doubt my mother would have allowed my father to hire you if she had known you would be just like your mother!" he sneered.

"What is that supposed to mean?" Becky raised her voice slightly. How dare he talk about her mother that way!

"Nothing. Only, I heard from some of the other servants that your mother was dismissed from working at Blairwick for being…how should I put it? Indecent?"

"How dare you? My mother stopped working to marry my father!"

"Not what I heard…I heard your mother had eyes for my father and probably for his money too! The head housekeeper had to dismiss her."

"I don't believe you," Becky said, her eyes flashed with fury. "Take it back, Edwin!"

"I did not really believe it entirely until I saw how you act around him!" Edwin shouted back. Just then, Becky decided she had enough of this foolish, spoiled boy. Without thinking, she slapped him in the face.

"Whoa, Becky! What's wrong!" she heard Charlie call. She got a hold of her temper and stepped back away from Edwin. Edwin rubbed his cheek, scowling.

"Go ahead, run to him like the little trollop that you

are," Edwin whispered. "Like mother, like daughter."

"What's going on here?" Charlie came over to both of them. He put his arm protectively between them, and looked dead center into Edwin's eyes. Edwin took a couple steps back.

"Nothing. Edwin just told a terrible lie, so I had to set him straight," Becky said, tears coming to her eyes.

"Apologize to the lady," Charlie said.

"She's no lady," Edwin barely said. Charlie reached over and yanked Edwin up by the collar. Edwin's eyes widened in fright.

"I said to apologize..." Charlie said.

"I will. I will. Just let me go," Edwin whined. Charlie held him a few seconds longer and then dropped his hold on Edwin.

"Sorry, Becky. I should not have called you that name," Edwin stuttered. He did not look up. He said the words and then took off down below.

"What did he call you?" Charlie asked.

"Never mind," Becky breathed. "Just forget about it,

Charlie."

"Only if you are alright," Charlie said. He placed his

hands on her shoulders. Becky stiffened as he did it. He lifted her

chin up. "Are you alright, Becky?" he asked, his blue eyes piercing

into her gray ones.

"Yes," she said. She stepped back. Perhaps some of

what Edwin said was true. Perhaps she had sent Charlie the wrong

idea and now out on the open sea, she suddenly got very scared of

the older boy.

Charlie stepped back too. "Got to get back to work then," he

mumbled. She just nodded and watched him walk away.

CHAPTER SIXTEEN

Down below, Becky found Edwin slumped in the corner studying Frankford Kendree's map and the book on Gibraltar. He did not glance up when she walked into the cabin. She decided not to talk to him either and went to her side of the room and closed the curtain, separating them. She sank on her bed and covered her eyes.

"Becky," she heard Edwin say rather tentatively.

She uncovered her eyes and rolled them. He cannot even keep quiet for a minute, she thought. "Yes," she answered.

"I am sorry for what I said about your mother and...about you,"

Becky was taken aback. She thought the apology earlier had been forced, but this one did seem genuine. She still sat on the bed, glad the curtain separated them still for now there were tears trickling down her face. She usually was not such a crybaby; however, the pain of the loss of her mother was made fresh by even the mention of her, especially such awful things about her that were clearly untrue, hurtful lies.

"I do accept your apology, but Edwin, why did you even say that to begin with? You should never listen to thoughtless gossip. Why say those words to me? Why do you insist on being so cruel? I may be a maid, but I have feelings too you know," Becky said. However genuine his apology, she was still enraged by what he had said about her mother.

"I said I was sorry, Becky. I had overheard things from the servants; and it started to make sense, why my mother did not like you from the start. She was upset by the rumors about your mother and my father. The rumors said he fell in love with her on holiday at Blairwick one summer, so she was dismissed. I do not think there was anything really to it, but my mother and father did get into a big row the week before your arrival, and that is when I heard all of the servants whispering. Mrs. Cackle does not have a very good whisper as you know. I heard her talking to Julie in the hallway one day about how my father was only seventeen and your mother sixteen the summer she worked there. My grandmother likes you and liked your mother, so I am sure nothing inappropriate had ever happened between your mother and my father, or she would have never allowed my father to hire you. Anyways, I am sorry, Becky." Edwin said. Becky did not respond to him at first. She had to let his words sink in. So that is why young Mrs. Kendree was out to get her from that first day? She still did not believe that everything he said was true, but it did leave her with a lot to think over. She would have liked to have kept pondering about it, but Edwin peeked through the curtain.

"Is there never any privacy!" Becky exclaimed, exasperated. She threw her pillow at him and quickly wiped her eyes. He caught it and grinned.

"Oh, I did so want this pillow! Thank you!" he said and went back to his side.

"Give that back, Edwin!" Becky rose from the bed and followed him over to his side of the cabin. She went after him and grabbed his arm to yank the pillow from him. He laughed. He swung the pillow over and knocked her with it.

This made her good and mad by now, so she was able to quickly grab the pillow back and return the favor, hitting him square in the face.

"Ouch, Becky! I yield," he said, laughing. She looked over and laughed at him too.

"Edwin, you are the most mercurial boy I have ever met," Becky said.

"What a big word for a maid to use," Edwin replied.

"Oh, Edwin! There you go again trying to keep me in my place. Why must you always point out my position? Are you really that insecure?"

"I am secure…look who can't stand being called a maid!" Edwin retorted.

Becky shook her head. "Well, you seemed to think I was pretty valuable this morning when I figured out the poem. Perhaps, you can learn a thing or two from this maid."

"Perhaps I already have," Edwin said. He went over and grabbed the map and the book of Gibraltar. "Here, finish reading this book, and I'll reread the map and poem. Then we can switch. By the time we reach Gibraltar we should have most of it memorized. How long until we get there anyway?"

"Four days," Becky said, "four more days of putting up with you." Just then, they heard a scratching on the door.

"Who is there?" Edwin asked, trying again to sound brave, but Becky could not help but catch the quiver in his voice.

No one answered. The scratching started again. Becky whispered to Edwin, "Open the door, Edwin. It could be Charlie."

"Alright, whoever you are, I am opening the door now," Edwin announced. The scratching continued. He opened the door quickly, but no one was there. "Well, I never," Edwin muttered and then Becky giggled. She watched as a brown tabby with white boots and a white bib rubbed up against his legs.

"Must be the ship cat," Becky said. She leaned over and called for the cat. He pranced by Edwin and jumped up on her legs, begging.

"Why the blazes do they have this cat wandering around?" Edwin muttered. "I wish Boris were here to teach it a lesson."

"Relax, Edwin. Every ship has a cat. It's bad luck not to," Becky said. She leaned over again and rubbed the tabby under its white chin.

"Well, we will need luck that's for sure," Edwin said. He walked over to the books and took up the map again, prying over it. Becky went back to her side of the room with the giant book of Gibraltar and sat down with her new friend, the ship cat. And there they sat for the remainder of the day, eating crackers for breakfast and lunch. They read until later that evening when Charlie came to them with some dinner.

After dinner, Becky said she would like to take a walk up on the deck. Charlie eagerly said he would join her, but when they asked Edwin, he just shrugged and said he would rather read and go to bed early. "Suit yourself, young chap!" Charlie said. "And I am glad that you seem to have treated Becky with a bit more respect since this morning." Edwin just glared at him in response.

"Be sure you do the same," he muttered out of earshot of Charlie, but Becky heard him as she followed Charlie out of the cabin.

Once on deck, Becky looked up at the stars, "Orion is bright tonight," she said, pointing to her favorite constellation.

"Yes," Charlie said. He leaned up against the rail. "And who taught you the constellations?" he asked.

"My father. We sometimes would sit out by the sea on a summer evening and all gaze at the stars together. Most of the other fisherman of the village would be in bed by then, ready to start the day early, but every now and then, father took that time to spend with us. He would say, 'It is too beautiful tonight to sleep. Let's go catch a shooting star.' The townsfolk thought we were odd, but none of us seemed to care. If we ever saw a shooting star, we had to make a wish then and there. But father told us to never say our wish aloud, or it would not come true."

"And did you ever see a shooting star?" Charlie asked.

"Yes, the night my father never came back home. I ran outside on the beach, my brothers with me. I saw the shooting star, but my brothers did not. They said my eyes were playing tricks on me, but I knew. I made my wish."

"And did it come true?" Charlie asked.

"No. I wished for him to come back, but he never did." Becky put her hand to her face to wipe away the small tears in her eyes.

"Ah, lass. I am so sorry," Charlie said. He stepped over and gave her a brief hug. She stiffened at his touch, so he drew back. "It is okay to lean on someone when times are hard," he said.

"I just feel so alone…and I am scared," Becky whispered. She gazed up at the open sky.

"Well, you are not alone now. And you know what I think, Becky. Just because you can't see your father, doesn't mean he isn't looking down on you." Charlie said. He looked her straight in the face, "And as long as you are with me, you are safe. There is no need to feel scared."

Becky nodded, "Thank you, Charlie. What about you? Where is your family?"

"Me? Why, I sprang from the sea!" Charlie smiled, deflecting her personal question. But then his eyes hardened some, "My mother sent me to work on a ship when I was twelve. I have been at sea for three years now and six months and four days."

"And your father?" Becky asked.

"Never knew him. But I have learned a lot from old Red here, and I've learned a lot from being on the sea and from gazing at the stars," Charlie quickly turned on a smile, but Becky knew this time it was forced.

"I am sorry too," Becky said.

"What for? The open sea is the life for me! My home is wherever the sails take me. Now, enough of my story. Are you going to tell me what you and Edwin are really doing?"

"Well...I better ask Edwin first," Becky said.

"Is that boy treating you fairly? I assume you don't slap boys in the face every day? He made you pretty upset, didn't he?" Charlie asked her, suddenly remembering this morning.

"Yes, he makes me upset, but it was just silly, really. He thought I was..." Becky paused not sure if she should tell him, "he thought I was flirting with you."

Charlie laughed and grabbed at his sides. "Did he? Well, tell that little Edwin that I am no competition. Besides, you are too young for me anyways!"

"I hardly see how it is so funny!" Becky flared. She was glad it was night time because her cheeks were bright red.

"I am sorry, lass. It's just plain to the whole crew that the boy likes you. The only reason he thought you and I were flirting with each other is because he is jealous. He is lovesick despite all of his attempts to tell us differently. I could see it when I first met you. I thought you had run away together but wasn't sure if you were having second thoughts about it," Charlie said.

"Edwin liking me? I think you are all daft. If Edwin Kendree is smitten with me, I will eat my handkerchief!"

This made Charlie laugh again. He had to cover his face from laughing harder, "You are really funny when you are angry."

This made Becky even more upset with Charlie, "And we most certainly were not running away together…we were running away from being kidnapped!"

"Kidnapped?" Charlie stopped laughing. "From who?"

Becky lowered her eyes. Should she tell him? As she was trying to decide, Charlie grabbed her arm gently, "Becky are you in danger?"

She looked up into his eyes which had hardened in anger. She whispered, "Yes."

"Then tell me everything," Charlie said.

"But…"

"But what? Becky, I need to know about the danger, so Red and the others will be ready. You can trust me," Charlie said.

Should she trust him? She wondered. She did feel so safe with him, as if she had known him all her life and yet she had been wrong before about people, about Zachery. "Yes, I trust you," she said. And as she said it, she saw something: a flash streamed quickly across the dark sky. A shooting star!

"Make a wish!" Charlie smiled. "I have made mine."

Becky wished again, but this time she wished to live with her brothers and sisters again. She wished for a place to call home.

"What did you wish for, Becky?" Charlie asked.

"If I tell, it won't come true," she answered and turned to him and smiled.

"That's right, I forgot," Charlie smiled too but then added in all seriousness, "Well, now that we have wished on a star together, tell me everything. Tell me, so I can help you make whatever that wish you made come true."

Without another thought, Becky confided in him what had happened. The secret tunnel. Hinistrosa. Being kidnapped. Gibraltar. Everything. When she was done, she glanced at him to see what he thought.

"Heavens above, Becky. What have you gotten yourself into?" he asked and then added, "I must admit, you are the most interesting girl I have ever met. One of a kind!"

"So...will you help us? Find the treasure?" Becky asked.

"Of course, you silly girl. Who wouldn't want to find long lost treasure?" Charlie jumped up suddenly. "I should tell Red that we might get some company along the way. And you, get back in that cabin...you never know if that Hinistrosa serpent will sneak up on us."

"Charlie!" Becky called after him, and he spun around quickly.

"Yes?"

"Please don't tell Red everything. About the map…and the treasure. I don't know if I can trust him…just you." she mumbled. She already felt bad for telling him so much without running it by Edwin first.

"Ah, lass. Nothing to fear with Red, and I will make sure to leave out the details to the rest of the crew too. No need to worry."

"Thank you, Charlie," Becky said, "for everything."

"You're welcome, Becky. And I meant it when I said it. You are safe with me."

He turned after he said it, and Becky watched the boy dash away. She glanced back up at the night sky, gazing for a long moment where she had seen her shooting star. This time, she dared to hope that her wish might come true.

CHAPTER SEVENTEEN

"Almost there!" Charlie shouted down the stairs into the cabin a few days later.

"Wonderful!" Becky yelled back. "Edwin, isn't that good news!" Becky exclaimed but Edwin was ignoring her as he did since she had told him about her talk with Charlie. He had been pretty upset that she had told their secret, and she was beginning to suspect that he was a bit jealous of Charlie too.

"Humph...Well, I guess it is good news for Charlie and Red and their men since they can take the treasure right away from us as soon as we find it," Edwin sourly said.

"Edwin! They would have found out regardless when we tried to sneak the treasure back on the ship. At least now we will have protection in the Rock's caverns. If you ask me, I am rather glad that some of them will be there in case Hinistrosa somehow has followed us," Becky said as she packed up some food in a small pail Charlie had given her.

"Well...it just was not right of you to tell them is all..." Edwin mumbled from his side of the curtain. Becky yanked open the curtain as soon as she was finished packing and stepped over him. As she did so she was very tempted to kick him, but she withheld that urge.

"Are you coming or should you give me the map?" Becky asked.

"Not going to give you the map that's for sure," Edwin said as he very slowly got up. "The map stays with me from now on…you would end up giving it to that McCoy chap while I wasn't looking."

"Oh please, Edwin," Becky said and rolled her eyes. "Let me have the map again. It was I who saved it from the journal. You know you can trust me." He looked at her then and slowly handed her the map. She looked him in the eye, smiled, and then climbed up the stairs, hearing him following her closely without saying a word.

Once up on deck, Becky gasped. Through the morning dawn, she could see the majestic site of the Rock of Gibraltar. It was purely magnificent. Golden and scarlet rays danced along the jagged shaped rock, illuminating it as they approached. She stood transfixed, watching the rock in awe, and deeply wished her father could have seen it. Then again, she thought, maybe he was watching just as Charlie had said.

"Meow!" Becky glanced down as the ship's cat took her gaze from the rock. Charlie had told her the crew had named him Henry.

"Hello, Henry boy," she spoke soothingly to the cat. The cat rolled around playfully on his back, sticking his white belly up.

"Best get that cat below," Charlie said to her, smiling though. "We don't want to give 'em a chance of sneaking off and giving us bad luck now."

Becky smiled back at him and shooed the cat back down the stairs and past Edwin, who was not looking quite as glum as he had just looked below. And when Becky had returned from setting up Henry the Cat like a king with food and water in the cabin, she noticed that Edwin had a smile on his face.

"We are here. We are really here!" Edwin exclaimed. He looked at her excitedly and then pointed at the Rock. They were getting even closer now.

"I know!" Becky was so glad that Edwin seemed to be in good spirits; it would make the day so much better without all of his gloomy comments.

Charlie came over to join them. "Well, Red says he will leave the other men on the boat but that he and I will go along with you."

At this, Edwin's eyes narrowed but Becky said, "That will be a relief. And one of the men will come get us if they spot anyone who looks like Hinistrosa?"

Charlie nodded a yes and then added, "Do you have any idea which cavern it might be in?"

"We'll tell you when we get there," Edwin answered before Becky could.

"Fair enough," Charlie said "Well, I need to get back and help Red and the boys get us into port!" he winked at Becky as he clapped Edwin on the back, something Edwin was none too fond of.

Becky stared as they approached one of the busiest ports she had ever seen. No wonder Gibraltar had been called the Gateway to the Mediterranean. She then whispered to Edwin the words of Sir

Frankford Kendree that had brought them to this place.

> "The key to the treasure awaits
>
> Lying at the old sea's gate.
>
> Find it near the majestic rock
>
> Where only the holy dare to knock."

Neither of them said anything else as they were soon overcome by the site and sounds of Gibraltar Port.

After they were docked, Becky and Edwin followed Red and Charlie off the ship. Of course, as they walked away from the ship, Becky felt less safe. At every turn, she felt uneasy, as if someone were watching them. The night before, she had had one of her dreams and could not sleep. She had ventured up on the deck and thought she saw an outline of a ship in the distance. Of course, she had wondered, what if it was Hinistrosa?

As they walked throughout the rather overcrowded, dirty streets, she stepped closer to Charlie for protection. She knew that Edwin was upset with her, but she herself was still glad that she had told Charlie about the treasure. She heard numerous accents and languages as they walked through and could not help but notice that several of them were extremely poor. Their living conditions looked similar if not worse than the poorest of London's slums. And the narrow streets were overcrowded with people with terrible smells of waste and sweat.

"How long will it take us to get to the caverns?" Becky asked Charlie.

"A good while," Charlie explained. "Plus, don't get too excited. If we don't know which cave to look in, we might be here a long time. There are over 100 known caves and many still are unknown. That's why I had you pack some food since we will be there all day…"

"Well, just how long are we planning on searching?" Red gruffly voiced. "I am not going to waste much of my time looking for this here childish fantasy."

"Well, but you promised…"Edwin squeaked.

"I know that boy!" Red exclaimed. "A few days and my ship goes back on course! I just want to let you know that, and if you do know which cave, then you better fess up now!"

"Red is right," Charlie said, he shrugged his shoulders and kept very lighthearted despite the fact that Red had been shouting.

"Well," Becky whispered to Edwin, turning to him. "We might as well tell them. If we hold out, we may get lost...or worse...we might give Hinistrosa time to figure out where we are."

"How would Hinistrosa know! No one knows about Gibraltar but us. But, I guess we better tell them or that Red will leave us in this filthy place," Edwin hissed back.

"It's in St. Michael's Cave," Becky said, "Or at least that's where we think it is, the part that is called Cathedral Cave."

"By Jove, that is all the way in the upper portion of the Rock!" Red practically shouted. "I hope you are ready to hike up to the entrance. We'll need to find ourselves a guide or something now."

"No guides!" Edwin shouted this time back.

"Hold on," Charlie said as he tried to calm down the situation. "Red just means we need to get a local to take us up to the cave's opening. They won't need to know why and won't need to go inside with us, right Red?" Red just grunted as his yes.

Becky nodded. She did not want to get lost and after all, she had read in the book about the Rock that it was over 1,300 feet high. It would take hours just to get up to the cave's opening.

"Well, you children wait here and get some more food, while I go and find us a local to guide us up!" Red stopped and pointed to a bench near a cheese shop. "And Charlie, don't let these ones run off without us. I can just see their skeletons being found in the caves if they were to run off alone. You know, grown men have gone in and have never come back!" Red seemed to be in a perpetual state of shouting out orders.

"Yes, sir," Charlie said as he nodded, a smile spreading across his face. He seemed to think the entire situation was a bit funny. Becky was beginning to get very irked with him.

"Well, what is the joke, anyway?" Becky asked him after Red had left and Edwin was buying more cheese.

"What?" Charlie asked, a twinkle of amusement in his blue eyes.

"You know….smiling and laughing off everything as if this is all just a joke," Becky said, her gray eyes flashing with fury.

"Well, I am sorry, but it is a bit silly. Chasing treasure and all. I do apologize though since you seem to believe there will actually be treasure there…" Charlie said, not taking the look of amusement off his face.

At this remark, Becky piped, "Is it so silly to believe, considering we were kidnapped for the treasure and are risking our lives now? I am sorry I even told you!"

This seemed to hit its mark, as the comment wiped away Charlie's smile, "I am sorry, you feel that way, lass. I didn't mean to make you so upset. I just don't think there will be anything up there…even if there had been buried treasure; it was probably found years ago is all."

She turned away from him, but felt his hand clasp around hers, "Becky, I am sorry. When I told you that night you could trust me, I meant it."

She did feel a sudden rush of warmth at his touch, and looked up and saw that he really did mean it; there was not a trace of a smile now.

"Charlie, I.." Becky started but was interrupted by Edwin.

"Oh, come on then! I think I see Red coming through the crowd." Edwin said hurriedly.

"Right," Charlie said and turned to exit the shop with Edwin. As Becky followed them out, she saw Red coming along with a dark haired man in rather ratty clothes. His dark eyes seemed to be looking in every direction but theirs.

"Well, this is the right man for us," Red said. "He agreed to take us up to the top of the Rock!"

From the looks of the shifty eyed man, Becky had her doubts, but if he was only guiding them to the entrance of the caves, then what could be his harm? Edwin seemed to share her doubts, "Looks like we need to watch this one," he whispered to her.

"You can't always tell by mere appearances, though," she whispered back.

"Well then, Julio, how long should it take to get us to the top with these children in tow?" Red asked.

"With a girl...possibly two and a half or three hours," The man named Julio said with a thick Spanish accent.

Becky quickly countered, "I am not a regular girl, sir. I am strong and not afraid of a good hike!"

Charlie let out a chuckle which in turn made everyone laugh as well. Their laughing only made her more furious, especially at Charlie.

"Good man, we will have to start right away if that is alright with you. Are the paths dangerous?" Red said in his gruff voice.

"No, senor. But beware of the monkeys on the climb," Julio said.

"Monkeys, you say!" Edwin said and laughed rather pompously, "I should think we are not afraid of little monkeys!"

"They do bite sometimes and will reach out and grab your belongings...hold onto your food," Julio said. Becky immediately drew her bag of cheese and bread close at which Charlie laughed again.

"Don't worry, lass. I shall defend you from the Gibraltar monkeys. How about I carry your food?" Charlie asked. Becky nodded. Monkeys? She had not read about the monkeys. What else would they discover about Gibraltar?

CHAPTER EIGHTEEN

"We are almost there," Julio the guide shouted back down to them. They had been hiking for about two hours. The guide, Red, and Charlie were out in front, and although Becky felt she could have kept up with them, she decided not to leave poor Edwin behind. He had been panting after the first hour.

"Good!" Becky shouted back to the guide and turned to Edwin, "Are you tired, Edwin? Perhaps we should take a break?" Becky asked.

"Never. I am not tired. I am only going at this pace to be with you...to protect you of course," Edwin said between heavy pants of breath.

"Of course..." Becky just smiled. Just this once, she held her tongue. She did not want to get in a fight with the boy...not when she felt sorry for him. She smiled to herself when she thought how they had all been worried about her, the girl, holding them back.

Becky and Edwin resumed their pace and Becky continued to

marvel at the sights of Gibraltar. The light gray rocky backdrop

actually held some rather lush green vegetation. And within that

vegetation, could be seen the Gibraltar monkeys everywhere. The

apes were cinnamon color. The guide said they were Barbary Apes

like the ones in northern Africa. None of them had approached

them yet, but she could see them creeping along and watching them

as they walked by. One young monkey in particular actually seemed

to be following them for the last couple miles. And even though

Julio had said to beware of them, Becky surprisingly did not feel

afraid of them, especially the small little traveling friend. He was

quite cute. A mile back, she heard Julio yelling at them, "Back

monos! Back!" So, in her mind, she kept calling the little one Moe,

short for the Spanish word for monkey.

She wondered if the little monkey Moe would follow them all

the way to the cavern opening. She secretly hoped so- she found the

animal quite charming.

"I wish we could give the little monkey food..." Becky found

herself saying to Edwin.

"What! Never! You heard the guide...besides, who wants that

foul little beast following us anyways," Edwin muttered.

Becky shook her head in frustration as she spoke, "Well, I rather like the little fellow. Moe! Here boy, keep up!" She thought she might be able to at least convince Charlie to give the little guy a morsel or so if he was still following when they reached the top.

Within a few minutes, Edwin and Becky joined the others at the opening to the caves. Julio, the guide, held out two lanterns for them as they approached. Becky quickly glanced over and saw that Red and Charlie both had theirs as well.

"Well, thank you, my good fellow," Red bellowed at Julio. "I am much obliged to you." The two men shook hands.

Becky turned and saw that her little friend, Moe the monkey was lingering just a few feet from them.

"Adios," Julio said to all of them. As he turned from the men, he seemed to follow Becky's gaze of the monkey. "Don't worry, I'll make sure the monkey will not follow you. You didn't feed it, did you?"

"No, although Becky wanted to," Edwin rapidly tattled. Becky rolled her eyes.

"Well, they usually don't follow so closely unless they want something you have. Take care now."

"You won't hurt the monkey, will you?" Becky asked, afraid of the answer.

Julio chuckled. "No, senorita, I do not hurt that which does not hurt me." With that, Julio turned and went back along the little path they had just come from.

Becky held onto her lantern tightly and her heart beat rapidly. "This is it," she whispered, "I know we will find it today!"

"Well, now who has the map?" Red asked suddenly and a little too gruffly.

Becky and Edwin looked quizzically at each other, not sure how much to say to Red. Becky spoke first, "We told you we think it is in St. Michael's Cave…Cathedral Cave. That is where we should start."

"Yes…but who has the map?" Red asked again. He stood there with a lantern in his huge, ruddy hand and a shovel in the other, and suddenly, Becky felt afraid of him. She glanced over at Charlie, who also was looking a little puzzled for a second.

"Ah, Red. If the children want to hold onto the map, let them. We can just go to Cathedral Cave and have a look around," Charlie said.

"Humph," was all Red said. "Waste of time, this is. Well, follow me. I don't want to have to live with losing any children on this fool hunt but if you run away, that is on you." With that, Red said no more and marched into the opening of the cave.

"Best keep up, lass. You too, laddie," Charlie added and followed Red into the cave.

"I have a bad feeling…"Edwin said, his voice cracking.

"Oh, everything is fine," Becky shakily whispered back and nodded her head to hurry him along. Despite the quiver in her voice, Edwin was determined not to be last, so he went on through.

Becky glanced back and saw the little monkey's light green eyes watching her in a lush patch of vegetation. "Goodbye, little Moe, you need to be our lookout." The little eyes just stared blankly back at her. Becky turned and held her lantern timidly in front of her with one hand, while lifting her skirt up with the other. And then she walked straight into the dark mouth of the cave.

Once inside, Becky patted the map she had kept with the poem inside her dress pocket. She only knew that they should be looking for St. Michael's Cave, in particular, the Cathedral Cave charted out in the Gibraltar book. She watched as the light of the lantern bounced off the brown walls of the cavern. She saw the three lanterns in front of her, and sped up, not wanting to fall behind.

"Stay a little back, lad!" Charlie chuckled and teased Edwin- the first to speak in the caves. Edwin seemed to be practically stepping on top of Charlie's heels.

"Keep close though," Red grunted as he marched along.

As they got deeper and deeper into the cave, Becky felt colder and colder.

Suddenly there was a turn in the cave with two paths. Red stopped and stooped down.

"What are you doing?" Edwin demanded as they watched Red

pull out rocks from his pocket and place them in an arrow formation.

"He's making sure we can find our way back is all," Charlie said calmly. Becky sighed with relief. She had been getting worried about getting lost inside this mammoth of a cave. In the back of her mind though, she wondered, if this was leading their way back, couldn't someone else easily just follow the path and find them? She pushed it further from her mind as they resumed their pace.

Several twists and turns and placing of rocks later, the four came into an enormous opening.

"I'll be," was all Red said.

"Now, we know why they call it Cathedral Cave, then, hey lassie?" Charlie exclaimed.

"This is it! This is it!" Edwin kept saying over and over.

All of them were shining their lanterns in front of them, and as Becky caught glimpses of the differing brown and gold and green stalactites hanging everywhere, she whispered, "It's beautiful."

"Aye, it is," Red said. And then he turned to her gruffly. "Now give me the map, so we can start digging." He had a hungry gleam in his eyes.

"Well, it doesn't say on the map exactly..." Becky said.

"Give it to me, lassie!" Red said and took two huge steps toward her.

Charlie stepped between them, "Hold on, Red. Calm down."

"I said, I want that map!" Red went to raise a hand to Charlie. Charlie backed off, shock written on his face.

Edwin stepped closer to Becky as Red approached her and grabbed her shoulders, "Listen here, girl. Give me the map, is all."

"I...I don't understand...I thought you were helping us..." Becky's voice shook with fear.

Charlie stepped up to Red and tried to calmly put a hand on his shoulder, "Red, what is going on?"

"Ah, boy, don't look at me like that. I want that map because I need to find the treasure. The deal was to follow these children...see where they go, and get the treasure for him! That's all I needed to do, and he promised me a new ship." Red said matter of factly. He looked down and loosened his grip on Becky's shoulders.

Charlie looked up at the big, burly sailor who had been like a father to him, disappointment written in his eyes. Red released Becky.

"The map, child," Red said as he held his hand out.

Slowly, Becky drew the map from her pocket and handed it to Red.

Red smiled for the first time all day, but when he unfolded it, his eyes turned to rage, "This isn't a map of the caves! Only of the Mediterranean! What use is this!"

Becky and Edwin looked at one another. Red turned furious, "I should just leave you in here. Search for yourself. This is all I need. This is all he wanted anyway. Hinistrosa will still pay me for this map and for following you little brats!" Red grabbed his lantern and shovel and walked away from them.

"Are you coming, Charlie?" Red asked over his shoulder.

Charlie said firmly, "No. Take the map. I told these two we would help them, and *I* plan on keeping my word."

Red turned. "Suit yourself. I'm going back to tell Hinistrosa's men. If I were you, I would come too. There's no use you kids becoming skeletons here looking for a treasure that probably does not even exist. Save yourselves because when I get back, Hinistrosa and his men will be coming here any minute, especially if they saw us leaving with Julio. Charlie, I don't want harm to come to you and the kids, so lead them back out safely and get out of Gibraltar."

"How, Red!" Charlie shouted and the chamber echoed. "How do we go when the one ship's captain I thought I could trust, sold out? How could you do it, Red?"

"I just could not pass up an opportunity Hinistrosa offered. You know business is bad, and I have always wanted a bigger ship. I spoke to some of Hinistrosa's men before we left Glasgow, not my favorite type, but they gave me more money than this pitiful English boy here was offering, so I had to take it. Easy payment. Transport some kids to wherever they want to go, and have Hinistrosa's men follow. It is just business and opportunity, Charlie. Like I taught you."

"Aye. Business and opportunity. What about honor and duty?" Charlie spoke almost in a whisper. Becky could see, even in the lamplight, that the older boy had tears welling in his eyes. Her heart felt for him, for he had received one of the worst blows life can give, the betrayal of a friend.

Red looked for a couple more seconds at Charlie and spoke not a word as he wandered back the way they had come.

They watched the large shadow of him slip farther and farther away.

"What should we do now?" Edwin whimpered.

With a clear, firm voice, Charlie said, "We dig!"

Becky nodded, looking at Edwin. "Yes, let's find what we came for," she whispered. Her words bounced off the enormous chamber as if the voices from the ancients echoed their agreement.

CHAPTER NINETEEN

For the next couple hours, Becky and Edwin took turns digging and holding the torch. Charlie, the strongest of the three, dug the entire time. Becky could not help but notice how the older boy dug as if he was attacking the dirt. There wasn't much speaking, save for an occasional whine from Edwin.

"We'll never find it," he moaned.

Becky swung the torch around the cavern, spying the towering stalactites and spotting several of the holes that Charlie and Edwin had done of the chamber. If this was Cathedral Cave, then where was the treasure? She racked her brain for clues from the poem to see if she had missed something.

"What will we do if Hinistrosa and his men get here before we find it?" Edwin whined. Becky just shook her head in frustration with the boy.

"Edwin, my turn to dig, you hold the torch and keep watch," Becky finally said after a sigh. She jumped down with Charlie in the hole that was being dug at the moment, and as she did she noticed a massive stalagmite a few yards in front of them jutting out from the floor. No wonder they call this Cathedral Cave, she mused. The stalagmite looked like a giant altar and the hanging stalactites like flying buttresses in the medieval cathedrals in England. She dug a little more and then glanced up quickly.

"Where only the holy dare to knock!" she cried, echoes bouncing off the caves. And what do the holy do she thought. They kneel! Charlie stopped his digging for a moment while Edwin looked in the direction she was staring at.

"The poem!" Edwin said. "Yes, we know…that's why we are in Cathedral Cave digging our graves…"

"Yes…but…the poem was telling us even more…" Becky pointed toward the massive stalagmite in front of her.

"Yes…another stalagmite…" Edwin said,

"But what does it look like to you?" Becky asked.

Charlie whispered, "Looks to me like a church altar…"

"You think so too," Becky could hide her excitement no longer,

"Help me up…that's it."

"By Jove, Becky, you're clever," Edwin said as the light began to dawn on his face.

Charlie had already jumped out of the pit and had reached a hand down to help Becky up. Becky clasped his strong hand.

"That's the spot, alright" Edwin exclaimed.

"Well, tis worth a try, lass," Charlie winked at Becky as he rolled up his sleeves and started digging right in front of the stalagmite.

Becky did the same; she could hardly contain her excitement. Thoughts of her father came to her as she dug, how she wished he were here for this grand adventure. But other thoughts flooded her mind too, fearful thoughts of Hinistrosa and his men.

"My turn, Becky!" Edwin stated matter of factly after she had been digging just a few minutes.

"In a little bit," Becky said with a bit of an edge to her voice, "I'm not tired…" and as she said it she heard a thud right next to her.

"I can't believe it, but I hit something," Charlie said excitedly.

"Edwin, bring the torch over my way, please, so we can see. Becky, come help me dig!"

"It's there…it's really there," Edwin mused as he stooped down and lowered the torch right above the spot.

Charlie and Becky continued to dig, and as they did, they noticed an old solid chest begin to appear. Within minutes, they had dug around the edges to reveal the elaborate chest.

"Well, get it out, then!" Edwin barked.

"It's too heavy right now, we need to dig around it some more," Charlie said. He looked up and grinned at Becky. "I can't believe it, lassie, I can't believe this crazy story is true…"

Eventually, Becky and Charlie were able to dig the dirt around the chest enough to try to lift it. "Becky, you get on that end to lift on the count of three," Charlie said.

Becky nodded but when he counted to three, she could only lift her side barely off the ground. The chest was extremely heavy.

"Edwin…set the torch down for now…"

"But where? What if it burns out like yours and Becky's did when we started digging?" Edwin questioned.

"Well…we might have to chance it, or else this beauty is staying put," Charlie retorted.

"What if Edwin just tries to help with one hand. I'm sure we can manage this side if he helps a little," Becky suggested.

"Or *I* could use both hands while you hold the torch," Edwin said.

"Let's just try it Becky's way first," Charlie ordered, and for once Edwin listened.

"Alright then," Charlie said. "One, two, three!"

This time it worked. The three of them lifted the chest out of the ground and onto the floor of the cavern.

The chest was ornately decorated with overlays of Spanish designs. The lock was in the shape of a compass rose and the two handles, though old, were still in pretty good shape except for being slightly corroded with time.

"Anyone have a key?" Charlie asked. Becky shook her head no. Edwin looked dumbfounded. All this way, and they never thought of the key?

"Well, how about a good ole standby…I'll just take the shovel and…" Charlie struck the lock which gave way immediately…due in part, to its corroded condition.

All three of them looked at the broken lock, and all three rushed forward to open the case. As the lid opened, Becky took in her breath. Within the old chest, lay a multitude of what looked like old pieces of eight and other Spanish coins. Lying on top of the coins, lay a beautiful round garnet necklace inlaid in ornate Spanish gold filigree.

"It's beautiful…" Becky reached out for the necklace.

"Aye, the gold is beautiful too!" Charlie exclaimed as he started to put some in his pockets.

"Easy now, this belongs to me, you know," Edwin said, "After all, Sir Frankford Kendree is my ancestor."

Becky looked up at him sharply, "Edwin, after all we've been through, you want it all to yourself? You promised me some of my

share…"

"Yes, that is true…I suppose…but it is up to my family to

decide how much both of you …" Edwin started but was

interrupted.

"Well, just remember that Sir Frankford Kendree took this from

the Spanish ships during the siege of Gibraltar which technically

should have gone to the Crown…to England." Becky said, reminding

him that his ancestor's treasure was not honestly made. "Besides,

let's just enjoy this, Edwin. We've come too far to spoil this

moment."

Edwin nodded although he still looked sour as he watched

Becky and Charlie sharing in the joys of the treasure. Becky looked

down at the garnet again and as it caught the torchlight, it seemed to

shine and sparkle, white light reflecting in the stone.

"It's a star garnet, lass," Charlie said as he came to kneel beside

her, "Put it on, whatever Edwin says, we would not have found this

treasure if not for you," he said gently. His piercing blue eyes sparkled much like the garnet in the light of the torch. Becky smiled at him, but as she was about to put on the necklace, they heard an eerie sound. The sound of clapping echoed throughout the chamber.

"Well done!" A gasping, growling voice spoke into the darkness. Edwin wheeled the torch around just as the old man stepped out of the shadows along with three other men. Hinistrosa smiled and let out a slow, creepy guffaw.

CHAPTER TWENTY

Hinistrosa chuckled at the three of them again, "How nice of you to do all of the hard work for me." Becky glared back at him in disdain. She glanced beside him to see that he had brought company. Their baldheaded Gus stood with him as well as Zachery. The other men must be back at their ship, she thought.

"Zachery, you and Gus grab the treasure chest. I'll keep an eye on these young creatures with this." Hinistrosa pointed his revolver at the three of them, lingering some on Charlie, "I see you found yourself a bigger friend. Just know, boy, I have this gun, and I have used it many, many times. Now, step to the side, there away from the chest." Becky looked over at Edwin who still was holding his lantern, although she could see the lantern swaying from his nervous hand. She reached over and grabbed his other hand and squeezed it reassuringly. As she stepped to the side, following orders, she noticed that Charlie had not budged.

"Do as he says, Charlie, please," she whispered.

Charlie stared directly at Hinistrosa for another few seconds, sighed, and finally joined them. Becky exhaled with relief. She was worried Charlie would try to be brave and get himself hurt or worse.

She still held the star garnet necklace in her hand, slipping it into her pocket. "Best give that to me, Becky," she heard a smooth, familiar voice say. Zachery had stepped beside them and held out his hand.

"Take it, then, Zachery. You've earned it along with your thirty pieces of silver," she said coldly.

"You mean, my thirty pieces of eight?" Zachery smiled at her then. All the guilt she had seen on his face when he had let them escape in Scotland was now gone, replaced only with greed. Zachery turned back to get the treasure chest with Gus, the two seemed to be struggling.

"Now, now, Charlie is it? Your friend Red was a good amigo. Gave me this map, see. And told me where I could find you. You look like a strapping lad, how about you give my boys a hand?" Hinistrosa asked.

"I'd rather not, sir. I'm a bit weak from all the digging,"

Charlie said sarcastically.

Hinistrosa did not seem amused. He pointed the gun at Charlie, "Not a question, young boy. You will do as I say, or I will bury you alive in here. No one would come for weeks, perhaps forever."

Charlie narrowed his eyes, but obeyed as he had no choice. He went over and helped Gus and Zachery with the chest.

"You," Hinistrosa hissed as he directed his gun at Edwin.

"Me?" Edwin's voice cracked back in return.

"Carry the lantern and lead us back. Follow that man Red's markings he left for us."

Edwin nodded. He led them back through the dark cave tunnels, followed by Becky and Hinistrosa with the others heaving the huge treasure chest behind them.

It was twilight when they finally emerged from the caves and stood at its mouth. Edwin, for fear of walking too far without permission, stopped until Hinistrosa joined them. Becky looked up at the lush vegetation, and thought she saw a pair of green eyes in the trees. "Moe," she called and sure enough, the same monkey who had watched them go into the cave, sat watching for them still.

"We'll wait here while the others bring the chest," Hinistrosa said and motioned for them to sit on a rock very close to Moe the monkey and his friends.

Becky looked up at the trees and thought of what Julio had said. It was a crazy idea but… she went ahead and took the chance, "I'm hungry," she whined to Hinistrosa. "Please, do you have anything?"

"Hah! As if I'd give you anything, you cheeky girl!" Hinistrosa said.

Becky looked down at her feet in defeat. She had thought she could feed the monkeys and then all of them would appear, giving her and Edwin a chance to get at Hinistrosa's gun.

"What I will do, is eat this apple right in front of you," Hinistrosa smiled sickly at them. It was the first time Becky actually thought the man was mad.

"You are a cruel one," Edwin said, barely audible, out of the old man's earshot.

Hinistrosa, took a bite into his apple, the juice trailing down his old, gnarled face.

Just as he bit into it, out of the tree jumped a monkey quick as lightning and snatched his apple straight from his hand. "You little devil! I'll send you where you belong!" Hinistrosa fumed. He aimed his gun in the air when just then, Moe, Becky's monkey, came swinging down and bit Hinistrosa on the wrist, causing him to drop his gun.

"Ahhh!" Hinistrosa yelled.

"Come, Edwin," Becky whispered. "Run!"

Becky dashed down the path. She hated leaving Charlie back there, but thought she could get help in town and come back for him. She glanced back and to her dismay saw that Edwin had fallen down in pain onto the path.

"Edwin!" Becky cried. She stopped on the path, wondering what to do. Just as she was thinking, she saw that Hinistrosa was about to catch up with Edwin.

"Go, Becky!" Edwin shouted. "Go, get help!"

Becky stood a moment longer. Should she abandon Edwin and Charlie, or should she stay? Hinistrosa helped her decide quickly enough, for he raised his gun to Edwin's head. "Not another move, senorita!"

"Don't try it!" Becky heard a familiar voice, Charlie's, from higher up on the path. She hung her head and returned to the others...so much for her grand escape that Moe the monkey had given her.

Hinistrosa chuckled unnervingly as she ascended back up to where everyone now stood. It was getting darker, and the sun was setting rather vibrantly in differing hues of bright tangerine. The scene, had she not been in such distress, would have been quite beautiful.

Hinistrosa kicked Edwin back toward Becky, "Back to your sweetheart then! Ha!" Becky glared fiercely at him but dared not say a word. Poor Edwin was trying to keep his composure, but Becky could see how terrified he was...after all, he had been held moments ago at gunpoint.

"No more nursery games, children. If one of you runs away again, I promise you, your friends will be the ones to pay…" Hinistrosa said, and then wheezed heavily before coughing.

"Just what do you plan to do with us? You have your treasure. Let us go," Charlie suddenly spoke.

"Well, dear boy, when I have the treasure safely on my ship, I will have no more need for you or for the little maid for that matter; however, I think I'll keep this one," he pointed and chuckled at Edwin, "as an investment until I can get out to more open seas…in case you were to report anything. If, for instance, you do, I can just very well…"

Edwin's lip started to quiver, so Becky swiftly said, "Don't worry, Edwin," she whispered.

"Too bad," Zachery said, suddenly standing beside her. "I would have liked the maid on our ship to do some of our cleaning and washing," he cruelly teased her.

Disgusted, she looked away from Zachery's brazen gaze.

"Well, we better hurry boys," Hinostrosa ordered. With that, the men grabbed up the old chest, and Becky and Edwin led the way, knowing there was a gun at their backs. Along the way down, Becky heard the noisy sounds of the monkeys, and she thought for sure that she spotted her monkey Moe. His green eyes and bright face stared out at her from his perch high above them on a stone ledge, the fiery sunset behind him. "Thank you. A friend who helps in distress is a friend forever," she whispered pensively.

Back down at the docks, the silvery moon shone over the black waters. Hinistrosa had Charlie, Gus, and Zachery carry the chest onto his boat he had acquired back in Glasgow…the one Becky had seen following Red's boat on their journey to Gibraltar.

"Becky, why do they only want me to stay with them? I don't quite understand," Edwin moaned.

"Because, Edwin, you are the only one Hinistrosa feels is worth anything. Perhaps, your father knows by now, and there is a search? If so, Hinistrosa will have you," Becky trailed off; she did not want to frighten the poor boy even more.

"I see. But what will they do with you?" Edwin asked. "We've come so far together on this…it's just…well…" Edwin stuttered, "I am worried for you."

Becky was shocked. Could Edwin really be more worried about her than himself? She smiled, with a new affection for Edwin. "Worried about me? Edwin, you should know by now that I can handle myself."

"No worries, laddie. She and Charlie are being allowed to come back with me!" a voice boomed at them, causing them both to jump. In front of them, stood Red.

CHAPTER TWENTY ONE

"No," Charlie McCoy said vehemently upon his return from carrying the cases. Red's face turned like his name, red with rage.

"Charlie Boy, come with me…or they might take you both along for Hinistrosa's ride!" Red spoke in his shouting kind of way. As he was shouting, something furry grazed her leg. She looked down to see the ship cat Henry leaning into her. Charlie noticed too.

"You see, even Ole Henry has jumped ship. Good luck!" Charlie said, the twinkle coming back into his eyes.

"Good luck? I am not the one who will need it. You best make up your mind, boy. Come with me or be forced to go with Hinistrosa!"

"How about neither! I am not going on either boat without a fight!" Charlie countered.

Gus, who had followed Charlie back, pulled out a gun. "Boss says we have to get everyone on board. Come with me now."

He held the gun not at Charlie, but surprisingly at Becky. Becky felt her heart begin to pound and her knees get weak. Henry the Cat growled.

"Leave her alone," Charlie said. Gus pulled the gun away from Becky.

"Take them all, then," Red suddenly boomed, "I don't want them. Not now."

Charlie glanced at Red. "Goodbye, Red," he said stiffly.

They had no choice but to walk toward Hinistrosa's ship, Henry the Cat following them blindly as if there was not a care in the world. As much as she liked the big cat, she shooed him away at the boat's landing, "Go, now, find yourself a nice rich merchant to give you all the scraps you need. Don't follow us. Go, no more cares now." She said. The cat meowed, but then slinked away when she stomped her foot toward him. Oh, if she truly could just cast all her cares of the moment on God, as the verses say and as her dear mother used too. But how heavy her cares seemed, even heavier than her tired legs, trudging aboard yet another ship.

Once they were tossed into the belly of the ship and left alone, Edwin whispered, "I'm sorry you didn't get away...I feel this is all my fault." She looked over at the boy, astonished again at his sudden worry for her.

"No. I wanted an adventure too...and the money," she whispered back, regret in her voice.

"I wanted the money for my family. I wanted my family together again," she dared to whisper aloud. She glanced sideways at Edwin and saw the surprise in his eyes with a hint, just a hint, of sympathy.

"You know something," Edwin said sadly, "I want to go back to my family too. I wonder what they must think by now. Pearl should have already told them...and Mr. Jeffries. This was so foolish...all of it. I am sorry about the treasure, maid."

""Treasure maid...that she is," Charlie interrupted their conversation for the first time.

Becky glanced at him as he added, "Don't worry. I will vow to help you get that treasure still. My solemn vow...as I said before, I won't go on without a fight."

"No," she whispered. "Please, we can't possibly do anything now…"

"No! I order you not to!" Edwin whispered harshly, "We just need to find a way to get away from these devils. Escape is the plan…no more treasure."

"Easy for a rich lad to give up on the treasure, but what about Becky? What about her family and the share you promised her? And…I wouldn't mind a bit for myself either," Charlie said.

"But…we are so outnumbered, what could we possibly do?" Becky interjected.

"One word, lass. Mutiny." Charlie replied.

"Mutiny? What? Look man, just how do we convince Hinistrosa's crew to mutiny?" Edwin scoffed. "I hardly think it possible."

"Not to mention it is crazy!" Becky added.

"Not crazy, not impossible. We offer money. We simply pay

the sailors more than Hinistrosa is offering…after all, it worked on

Red. It could possibly work on these others. As I said before.

Mutiny. We take over the ship and let Hinistrosa and his right hand

men switch places with us."

CHAPTER TWENTY TWO

As they were whispering to themselves about Charlie's dangerous mutiny plan, they were joined abruptly by Zachery.

"Hinistrosa wants Edwin to be kept upstairs in a separate cabin. He's to come with me," Zachery said while looking them all over, his eyes resting on Becky. Becky frowned.

"Why?" Charlie countered.

Zachery sneered at him, "No concern to yours. I expect, like all things, Edwin is worth more than you both: a ship boy and a maid can hardly fetch a price. I wonder, if anyone even cares that the two of you are gone?"

Charlie stood up next to Zachery, "And what is that supposed to mean!" The twinkle and carefree nature was gone from Charlie's eyes.

"I don't take a liking to your tone, boy!" Zachery countered, shoving Charlie.

"And I don't like the likes of you shoving me and getting away with it!" Charlie said and punched Zachery square in the face.

Zachery's eyes widened just before striking back at the boy. Charlie

doubled over, and right as Zachery was bending close to strike again,

Becky ran and tried to hold his arm back. Zachery flung her aside,

casting her against the wall. Becky grabbed her side in pain as Edwin

came to help her up. Zachery gave Charlie another jab but Charlie

kept coming. He probably would have won the fight, but two of

Hinistrosa's men had arrived to drag Charlie off. As he was being

dragged off, Becky's hope seemed to be going with him along with all

of their plans.

Zachery, with bloodied nose and mouth just glared at her and

Edwin, "Edwin is to come with me. Upstairs. Now, Becky, the

question is what is to become of you?"

"Please, let me go..." Becky pleaded but her eyes flashed

with anger.

"No, but I don't like you down here...not with all these

sailors about," Zachery flipped back almost into his old self, or

rather, the person she thought she knew before all of this kidnapping

business. Becky kept her mouth shut as Zachery gripped her arm and escorted her away. "I guess you are happy, now? You would be

back safe at Kendree Hill if you had kept your place and not tried to

befriend your young master and mistress. You forgot the first rule:

they are not our friends." Zachery sardonically said as he pushed her

into a small cabin. Becky heard a thud of the door. Becky fell to her

knees. She was utterly alone. The room felt damp and the air humid.

It was more like a closet than a room. No windows, nothing but a

few bookshelves lining the walls. Her hope seemed dashed, and she

slowly began to cry. She thought of her home and of her brothers

and sisters. She dreamed of seeing them again. Her older brothers'

smirks, her beloved sister Susannah, her sister Katie's giggle. She

wanted to hug her little brother, rock her baby sister Lisbeth and sing

them the songs of her mother. She closed her eyes and imagined

them, but soon she couldn't. They faded away from her mind and

drowned in the darkness of the room. The only thing to do was pray

for a way out of the dark.

What seemed like hours passed, when she heard shouting on the

deck. Loud voices and chaos broke out. Becky was about to peer

out of her door, when Charlie swung it wide open. "Becky, you will

never believe it! A ship has caught up to us. They just shouted that

Hinistrosa and his men need to give up the ship or there will be a fight!"

"But...how did you already get free?" Becky asked. She was so puzzled by the sudden turn of events.

"Let's just say...I was already friends with some of the men on board!" Suddenly, there was a fire and crack of cannons lighting up the sky. Becky gasped at each horrid sound.

"But, Charlie, who is it...suppose they want the treasure too?" Becky stated one of her newfound fears.

"Then hang the treasure! We at least can get rid of that Hinistrosa!" Charlie shouted, and it was then she noticed it. He had a revolver in his hands. He glanced at her, with a worried look, "Here," he said, "take this. For your protection! I'll get another from one of my friends aboard. Besides, I have this too." And then Charlie showed her a sword hanging at his side. "I'll be right outside your door..."

After he left, Becky suddenly worried about Edwin. What would happen to him during the fight? Within minutes, she heard the shouts. It seems, Hinistrosa was not giving up the ship and treasure without a fight! Then, she saw feet underneath the door shuffling back and forth as if in a massive duel.

"They're here," Becky groaned. She heard swords clashing against each other, and suddenly she heard a familiar voice yell. It was Charlie's. She ran from the room and flung the door open. She saw Charlie on the floor of the deck about to be stabbed by a huge, burly man, Hinistrosa's goon named Gus. She pulled up the revolver with clammy hands and fired…and missed terribly. The sword came down towards Charlie, but she suddenly saw the other sailor fall over. Charlie had kicked his legs from under him. Soon another sailor, one of Charlie's friends, came over and finished the fight. Becky glanced around, her hands still shaking from shooting the revolver.

"Thank you, Becky," Charlie moaned.

She saw then that he had been wounded. A man of Hinistrosa's suddenly appeared. "Give me the gun!" he growled.

She flashed her eyes in defiance, so the man came over and held his knife up to her throat. Her heart pounding, she dropped the revolver. The man just sneered and seemed about ready to do her away when a crack rang through the air. The man slumped to the ground. She looked over and saw that Zachery Perkins stood with gun in hand. He had saved her life. Becky's eyes widened but there was no time for words. Zachery picked up Charlie and carried him back to her small room.

"Thanks," she mumbled as he left. Zachery said nothing, but just ran his fingers through his hair and turned again to leave. Becky stared after him for just a second before springing into action to help Charlie. He seemed to have been stabbed in the arm. She knew nothing about nursing but knew at least she had to stop the blood. She ripped part of her dress in order to make a tight bandage for him. "You'll be alright," she told Charlie over and over.

"But you won't be!" She heard a raspy chuckle coming from behind her. It was Hinistrosa himself, his old, glazed over brown eyes narrowing in anger. She whirled around.

"You, children, cost me my treasure!" his thick accent slurred.

He started to come towards her.

"You harm them, and I'll kill you myself!" a deep voice yelled. Sir James Kendree stood in the doorway. Hinistrosa turned around with a smirk on his face.

"You...gasp...you think you could kill me?" He swung his sword around, and he and Mr. Kendree began a sword fight right there in the tiny room.

"I'll go for the gun," Becky whispered to Charlie who nodded through the pain in agreement. Suddenly books flew into her as Hinistrosa knocked a bookshelf over, preventing her from getting his gun. Kendree knocked a chair at Hinistrosa in response which made the old man fall to the floor.

"You are now my prisoner! Do you yield?" Kendree's deep voice demanded.

"Yes!" Hinistrosa gasped, but just as he said so, Becky saw him grab for a knife in his pocket.

"Watch out!" she screamed, and Mr. Kendree dodged the flying knife just in time. Mr. Kendree punched Hinistrosa and hit him with the handle of the sword, knocking him unconscious.

Just then, a sailor came by and said, "Are you alright, Kendree? We found your son locked in the captain's quarters. He seems to be alright by the sound of it."

"Yes, I am fine. Take me to my son!" Kendree smiled in relief at hearing news of his son. "Take this man Hinistrosa along with the others to Inspector Stephens. And, it seems this young man needs a better bandage. Get someone to take a better look and clean out his wound." It was then that Mr. Kendree looked at her, "Come with me, child. Let's go find my son."

CHAPTER TWENTY THREE

Boris the dog guarded the locked door to Edwin's cabin but did rise up upon seeing his master. Becky watched as Mr. Kendree worked on breaking the lock.

"Hello, old boy!" Becky said, as the dog slobbered her hand and dress cuff. Mr. Kendree was easily able to break the lock.

"Edwin!" Mr. Kendree exclaimed and scooped his son up into his arms. "My foolish boy!"

At the word foolish, Edwin hung his head in shame. "I...I am sorry, father. I let you down. I should never..."

"I know, son. I know everything. Pearl and her little friend made it to Kendree Hill safe and sound...which is how I was able to procure a ship, along with Inspector Stephens. It was Inspector Stephens who was able to figure out from witnesses that you had boarded onto one of two ships...this one and another ship captained by a man who goes by Red."

"Sir, the treasure..." Edwin started but stopped himself. He seemed embarrassed to ask after all he had put his father through.

"Ah, yes, you mean the treasure that does not belong to us?" Mr. Kendree said rather sternly but then upon seeing his son's red face, said softly, "We are turning that in as well...for Sir Frankford Kendree was, as you know now, a pirate...a shame to our name."

Edwin nodded, "Yes, of course...Again, father, I am sorry."

"And as I said before, I know. Lesson learned, my son. Lesson learned. Let us not speak of it anymore. For all is well! And you, my dear son, are safe!"

Becky observed them, father and son, embrace again. Her heart was happy for Edwin, for it seemed, he had something more important than even treasure...he had a father. As she smiled, she also thought of her wish...of her family being together. The wish slipped away along with the knowledge that none of the treasure was hers, and rightfully so. Still, everything, this whole adventure then did seem such a waste. She supposed that sometimes there is no sense to some journeys, but at least the journey had ended and all could be as it was before.

Before she left them, she did manage to ask, "Sir, has anyone checked to make sure my sister is doing well? Hinistrosa threatened to hurt her…"

"Yes, my dear," Mr. Kendree turned to her, "And she is safe at Kendree Hill. I had a carriage sent for her as Inspector Stephens left some of his men to protect the estate. I thought it best she should leave that terrible factory."

"Thank you, sir. But what about her position? I am so sorry to have been mixed up in all of this. I cannot imagine how much grief this has caused to so many." Becky gushed. She was so very sorry for so much; especially, for her own greed.

"Nonsense. You are not to worry anymore. As for your sister's job, well, I have thought a lot about it, and I do so wish that your sister should leave that awful factory and stay on at Kendree Hill…or at Blairwick Manor even. My mother, at her age, wishes to retire to our country estate, and I am sure Jeffries will be in need of plenty of help."

Blairwick, the beautiful estate in Scotland where her own mother had once worked! Becky could barely contain her relief that dear Old Mrs. Kendree would take good care of Susannah. She was so excited, "Thank you, Sir! Your kindness is truly appreciated! My sister will do well there. It is such a magical place." And Becky would have gone on, speaking of it, but decided she was talking too much again. A simple thank you would have been more appropriate.

Mr. Kendree smiled and his eyes grew soft and reflective, "Yes, well, your dear mother was very kind to us, and it is the least I can do to make sure her family is taken care of. I will also write your aunt again and inform her of your safety."

At the mention of Aunt Matilda, Becky frowned slightly, "I do not think she would care..."

"Nonsense. I am sure your aunt cares for you all. She might be a bit overwhelmed about taking on so many children..."

"Sir," Becky dared to interrupt. "But I do not think...I mean..." she stammered. Suddenly, Edwin had found his voice again, and she heard him saying:

"Father, what she wants to say but can't is that she wishes to have her family all together again. That is what she wants more in the whole world…more than anything. That's why she followed along with my foolhardy plan. She wanted the treasure not to be rich…just so she could get her family back." He smiled looking at Becky, "Is there anything that can be done for them?"

Mr. Kendree knitted his eyebrows together and then clapped his son on the back, "My dear boy, perhaps this adventure has taught you more than one valuable lesson. I shall see what can be done for you, Becky. Your older brothers have a decent trade as sailors, and as I said, I shall make sure I take care of Susannah as well as you. Perhaps, you can go with your sister to Blairwick. Yes, I am not sure, but I will discuss it with my mother. Perhaps, when your younger brother and sisters are a bit older, they too can join you there. Or…perhaps…" Mr. Kendree drew thoughtful, "Perhaps, you and your sister could have the tenant's cottage on the property there. I could arrange for you and your sister to take turns working, so one could stay home with the younger children whilst the other one works. Yes! I do believe that is an option, and I daresay my mother would love it. She is, as you have discovered, a most charitable creature. How does that sound, my brave girl?"

Becky could barely speak. If what he said could actually happen, then her dream of her family coming together was already blossoming into a reality. She smiled, "I should say, that sounds splendid...and unbelievable, sir. I would be most indebted to you."

"Very well! Good! Good! Well, my dear, boy, I will leave you to talk with your new friend. I am going to see Inspector Stephens about what is to be done about Hinistrosa and his men. I must say, I never suspected Zachery, as my valet, to be involved with that lot. But, I suppose, one just never knows in these matters," Mr. Kendree turned to leave. Becky spoke up then.

"Please, sir. Do tell Inspector Stephens something for me. Zachery...he saved my life in the end," she stammered.

"Well, I shall tell the Inspector everything. You are right to tell me. I am glad the chap acted decent in the end. It does give some hope for the poor character. Still, I do not think it will expunge his other actions. We shall let the law decide. As for myself, I shall be looking for a new valet." Mr. Kendree replied and turned to leave.

"One more thing, father," Edwin added, "Can we do something for that little street urchin Loopie? Her family is at a workhouse...and I am told that it is deplorable," he stopped and looked over at Becky who already was beginning to feel ashamed that she had not thought of their young friend first.

Mr. Kendree nodded slowly, "Why, yes, my boy...I shall look into it when we return." And then Mr. Kendree said something Becky thought Edwin had been waiting a long time to hear, "And I must say, I am proud of you, son. Certainly not for this treasure business! But, I daresay, I admire your newfound charity."

"Thank you, sir," Edwin smiled. Father and son nodded to each other. Mr. Kendree turned and left.

Becky ran over to Edwin, "Thank you, Edwin. My family is getting back together...because of you!" Impulsively, she threw her arms around him in a huge, bear hug.

Edwin stiffened at her touch, "A maid is not supposed to just fling themselves into their employers, you know!" He backed away, turning red.

"Well, I guess you haven't changed that much…" Becky retorted. She too, stepped back.

"Calm down. I don't just consider you a maid anymore. I…I consider you my friend even if we do argue a lot," Edwin said slowly.

Becky smiled, "Edwin," she said, "Although I find you to be…a bit of a snob. I do consider you a friend as well. Friends?" She reached out her hand this time, knowing he would feel more comfortable with a handshake.

"Friends," Edwin said and shook her hand rather firmly. He always wants to prove himself. Becky just laughed.

"Well, we might not have gotten the treasure, but…at least we got an adventure!" she joked.

"Yes…and at least we have this…" Edwin said, looking from side to side, he took something out of his pocket.

"The Star Garnet!" Becky exclaimed, clasping her hand over her mouth in astonishment.

"But your father said we need to give it back!" She gasped as he swayed the brilliant necklace in front of him, grinning.

He said thoughtfully, "Hinistrosa had it just dangling out of his pocket. He was in here with me, questioning me when we first heard the shouts outside. He jumped up quickly, and it fell from his pocket. And I thought. Well, I thought, at least I have this. Please don't tell father…I plan to keep it. Maybe when I am older, I will sell it…to repay father for the money I took from him."

"I won't tell, Edwin. It is such a beautiful necklace! I suppose it will be our little secret. And our trophy! But, please, don't sell it." As she gazed at the brilliance of the star garnet necklace, she thought of the real star she had wished on. Thinking of the star, she suddenly thought of Charlie. "Goodbye, for now, Edwin. I need to check on Charlie! But thanks…for everything!"

CHAPTER TWENTY FOUR

Becky stood next to Charlie, who had his arm wrapped in a nice bandage now and was leaning over the rail, staring at the waves. "I do wish you would come to Kendree Hill with us," she voiced.

He looked at her a long time and smiled his huge, mischievous smile at her, "Aye, my bonnie lass. I know you do. But you see, land is not for me. I already talked with the captain of Mr. Kendree's ship. He says I can stay on with him, even with this lousy arm of mine. I guess I will be part of a new crew." He paused, "Never been on a ship without Red before. He…he was the only friend I really had in this world. And…" he stopped. Becky could see he was still hurt and angry.

"But you have to go with us! We are your friends now. I am sure Mr. Kendree will help find you a job and…" But Charlie stopped her.

"But my home is the sea! Can't you see, Becky, I don't belong anywhere else. My home's the sea; my life's the sea…" He said but then went silent.

Becky did not want to say goodbye to him. She did not reply. She could not stand that she would never see him again.

"Well, say something, Becky. Don't be mad! Maybe I'll write you," he paused and laughed, "Don't be so bull headed! Such a little fighter!" He said and jabbed playfully at her with his good arm.

"But Charlie! I am sure Mr. Kendree could help you find another line of work, as I said. They don't need the treasure; they are so rich...and generous too. Come stay and then figure it out..." she tried desperately to plead with him.

"But Becky, I don't need Mr. Kendree's money or another line of work. I have found my treasure already. My treasure is the sea! Becky, there are unsearchable treasures in life. You can search and find wealth, but you might never find happiness. My life and happiness is for the sea! It's what I am made for!" Charlie finished and Becky went silent. She put her arm around him then, for she did understand the pull of the sea on one's heart.

"Goodbye then, Charlie McCoy," she whispered.

The two of them stood silently on the deck, looking for another shooting star. Some friendships are formed on earth, and yet some are formed on shooting stars. And it was at that thought that Becky knew. This would not be the last she had seen of Charlie McCoy, and it would not be her last shooting star either.

Becky thanked God for her last wish coming true. Like Charlie had said, real treasure is that which is unseen, that which gives true happiness. And although she had been seeking earthly treasures, her treasure had been right under her nose. Her treasure was her family. And with the help of a shooting star, her new friends, and Mr. Kendree's kindness, she would soon be able to hold that treasure again.

CHAPTER TWENTY FIVE

In her dreams that night, Becky dreamed of a little gray stone cottage nestled among bright green hills. She and her brothers and sisters stood in an old doorway, waving goodbye to their parents. Her parents disappeared among the purple and blue flowers, swirling through the mists over the hills… somewhere where heather and heaven meet.

ABOUT THE AUTHOR

After working for eight years as a librarian, Kendra Dartez decided to stay home with her two adorable children until they are a little older. The idea of *Treasure Maid* came to her first as an eleven year old girl. The first draft was completed when she was in high school; however, it was not until just recently that she decided to come back to it and rewrite it. It is with great pleasure to finally realize her eleven year old dream. She enjoys reading, writing, singing, traveling, taking pictures, being active in her church, playing pretend with her kids, and playing sports with her family. She lives with her husband, her two children, and several books in King William, VA.

Made in the USA
Charleston, SC
20 December 2014